Adventures of the PPA: Invasion

Alan J. Duin

Copyright © 2017 Alan J. Duin

All rights reserved.

ISBN: 1976106656
ISBN-13: 978-1976106651

DEDICATION

This story was made possible through the support of all my friends, teachers, mentors, and my mother. I dedicate this story to my friends for all the years we've been together. In essence, they really are my dream team. You guys are awesome!

CONTENT NOTICE:

The content within the story **_is not_** suitable for all ages. The minimum age to read is 13.

Content includes:

- Mild to moderate action/sci-fi violence
- Mild to moderate language
- Mild suggestive dialogue

In other words, this novel is rated **PG-13**.

ACKNOWLEDGMENTS

Thank you to my mother for being there for me...

Thank you to my dear friends, Chris, Marc, Charles, Bill, Mike, Evan, Laura, Rebekah, and Jason for their support and being awesome...

Thank you to Donna for helping me edit my story and for being a mentor...

Thank you to my High School English teachers, Mrs. Carden and Mr. Goldman, for inspiring me to write creatively...

Thank you to my English teachers, Mr. Verdi and Mr. Moran, for keeping the Author's Club going and inspiring many students to enjoy reading and writing...

Thank you to Mike Swedenberg for being my writing mentor...

...and a big thanks to *you* for checking out my book!

IMPENDING CHAOS
I

At 30° Latitude, 60° Longitude, there lies a mysterious island in the Atlantic Ocean called Anthronia. It had been occupied by beings exiled from society ever since the dawn of human civilization. These beings may be commonly seen as monsters from a human's eye, but, despite looking different, are as equal to humans as humans are as equal to them.

The island natives consisted of multiple anthropomorphic races. One particular race on the island are the Najanians, reptilian humanoids with the anatomy and intelligence of a human. In addition, they also had other reptilian characteristics such as slit pupils in their eyes, slightly longer canines, and a lizard-like tongue.

One Najanian, in particular, is the owner of a company named S. C. Kharaab, Corp. He was a wealthy man given unlimited funding from Anthronia's leader. His company was involved with weapon and science research. There had been rumors about genetic experimentation going on, however, there is insufficient evidence to prove this.

For the past few years, this Najanian had plotted against the human world. One evening, he brought together five individuals who would help him devise such an evil plot. These individuals sat around a table in a meeting room with the leader of Anthronia.

The plan was to unleash an assault upon human territory, capture every last human, and cage them. Upon completion, they would take over and utilize the humans accordingly. One of the individuals said he would gather together his best warriors and others willing to invade. The second person said he would acquire the necessary vehicles and equipment for this operation from an extraterrestrial source. The third said he would pinpoint locations to hold the humans after they're captured. The fourth said she would retrieve special cages to hold the humans in. The fifth said he would acquire extra supplies.

    This diabolical plan was going to change the lives of not only the people around the world but change the lives of a group of teenagers from Levittown, New York. Of course, this group would never expect such a horrible thing to happen to them… and survive. These teens may appear normal to the eye but each one had their own skill.

    Within this tale, we will experience their adventure through the eyes of Alan, most of the time, since he is the one who leads his friends on an adventure to save humanity. Let us join our heroes to be and witness what they're in for.

Here we go…

HANGIN' OUT
2

It was the middle of April and spring recess had begun. Being off from school made everyone feel refreshed and alive. I was with my friends Marc, Chris, Bill, Evan, Rebekah, Laura, and Jason. We decided to get together since we never had much time anymore. Schoolwork became excessive and we had final exams in June. In addition, a lot of us were graduating from high school. Having this day to be with my friends eased the stress and anxiety.

Marc was working on a computer over at his work table. He liked to tinker with them, collecting spare parts, and using them to make his own system from scratch. His skill comes in handy when there is anything related to electronics or technology. It's always good to have someone like him around in case a computer goes berserk.

Chris was sitting on the far side of the basement. As an analytical and logical person, whenever I made plans or came up with an idea, the first one to spot an error and offer a solution to the problem, was him. His help had always made things work out for the better. In addition, he had always been a friend I could talk to whenever I had to get something off my chest.

Next up is the comedian of the group, Bill. Not only did he have a sense of humor that can make anyone laugh, he, too, was into videography. He brought a small camcorder with him everywhere. If he saw something he could use for his projects, he'd film it on the spot. He currently has it out, filming the entire basement and zooming in on me while I'm narrating…

Anyway, Evan was on his cell phone, probably texting some girl from school. He's a tall and strong guy able to lift two-hundred pounds with little effort. If we needed to move something heavy, just call in the human tank and he'll do the rest.

On the couch were the girls. Rebekah was on her phone texting friends. She, too, is capable of lifting heavy objects just like her brother, Evan. One thing to note is her short temper. One wrong move and you'll need an ice pack between your legs.

Laura, the youngest in the group and Marc's sister, was checking her makeup. A sweetheart by nature, she always wanted to be a nurse and help people. She may seem cute and innocent on the outside but this girl can hold her own in any situation.

Jason was sitting on the recliner reading a story I wrote called "Legend of the Lizard Man." He's a logical thinker by heart and does quite well in math and social studies. One time, he helped me prepare for a math Regents exam. The guy knows his stuff and I learned a lot from him.

Mike and Charles, two other friends who usually hang out with our group, could not join us today. Their parents wanted them to help around the house and do some spring cleaning. Even though we were two people short, we still had a good time.

"Alan, your stories are so bogus. Come on, us fighting monsters? Write something else that doesn't involve us fighting aliens or demons or lizard people," said Jason.

"Well, that's what I write. I like writing sci-fi adventure stories."

"I think those video games are getting to your head."

Jason had a point in some way. Even though I do get inspired by video games, writing, in general, had been therapeutic. I've been through a lot in my life. I was bullied plenty of times in school, and just a year ago, my father passed away. Writing stories was an outlet. It helped ease the pain.

"Alan, how about you write something like a story about teen struggle or something realistic?" said Rebekah.

"It's kind of hard to think of something with that theme. Writing fiction is easier for me," I replied.

"Of course, because your mind is focused on those video games all the time," added Jason.

"How about doing something else other than playing those games and writing stories," said Rebekah, changing the subject.

"Yeah, man – Play some sports like basketball," said Evan.

"Well, I try to diversify my hobbies and interests but I just get so involved with my work."

"So, what are you working on now?" asked Jason.

"I'm working on a story. I'm nearly finished with it and hopefully, I can get it done today. I may need some concentration right now or I may lose my train of thought."

"Heads up guys, Al's in the zone," said Marc.

"How's it going over there, Marc?" asked Laura.

"Doing alright, I guess. I've been trying to give this computer a bit of a tune-up. This baby's got a hard drive space of over sixty-four gigabytes and a RAM of five hundred and twelve megabytes. It's a start but, with the parts I have, this is what I made."

"Marc, you are such a geek."

"Look at yourself, four eyes."

"You're so mean."

During this time, Chris walked over to Jason to look at my story. Jason was just about finished with it and looked displeased.

"Hey, J, can I read?"

"Yeah, you can read it. For some reason, I keep getting killed in Alan's stories then wind up being brought back to life in the next then wind up dead again."

"You did ask Alan to kill off your character. I do admit it is kind of funny."

"Yeah, hysterical."

Chris took the story from Jason and flipped to the cover. He analyzed it for a second and turned to the first page.

"Let's see, the name of this is Legend of the Lizard Man. Alan, didn't you want to make a movie of this a while ago?"

"The Legend of the Lizard Man? Yeah, I wanted to, but it didn't come out the way I planned."

Back when I first wrote the story, my friends looked at it and I asked them if they wanted to turn it into a movie. We tried and I made a whole lot of props for it. Unfortunately, the mask I created for the lizard man costume wound up under something in Evan's backyard and it got crushed. Sadly, the movie was never completed.

"Hey, maybe we can make a movie. Maybe not with a lizard man but something relating to your other stories," said Bill.

"What about that 'Invasion' one that you're working on? It sounded interesting," said Marc.

"I don't know. It's kind of a large-scale project. You would have to use a lot of CGI to render legions of creatures," I replied.

"Good point. What do you think we should make, Bill? You got any fun ideas up your sleeves?" asked Marc.

Bill checked his sleeves and replied, "Hmm... I don't see anything interesting in my sleeves. They're kind of empty – I only see my arms."

"Bill, I know you love whacking people with bats in your little videos like you did with Matt in that baseball skit. Maybe you should do something with a whole lot of slapstick," I said.

"That's definitely an idea. Good times remembering that skit. Beating Matt with a bat was sure fun," said Bill.

Bill loved to make funny videos in his spare time. He always practiced with silly little skits to improve his editing skills and any special effects he's testing, like explosions. His videos were always fun to watch. I myself nearly suffocate from laughing hard.

Things went alright until we noticed the lights flickering. We paused and waited to see if it flickered again. A moment later, the lights flickered more frequently. We were curious as to why they behaved this way. I looked around the basement and everyone was just as concerned as I was. Something did not bode well with me.

THE BEGINNING OF THE END
3

We all looked at each other. I closed my laptop and went to get Marc's radio in his office.

"Let's see if there's anything on the local news about a power problem," I said.

I turned the dials a few times to get a signal. There was a lot of static on many of the stations. Finally, I found one loud and clear. The anchor came on with breaking news.

"Ladies and gentlemen, we bring to you breaking news. The government has issued a national emergency. It has come to our attention that several unidentified flying objects are hovering above the entire United States. Reports also have indicated large numbers of U.F.O.'s being seen in other parts of the world – Wait, I'm now receiving word that smaller ships have been deployed and are dropping off these strange creatures. The creatures are now attacking everyone and causing destruction. Police and military units have been dispatched. Please seek shelter immediately. Lock your doors and windows. Remain inside until further notice."

"Are they serious?" asked Marc.

"They got to be joking, man," said Evan.

We started to hear sirens outside. A sense of dread filled the air. The anchor got back on.

"We've just received news that the unknown invaders have attacked many cities and annihilated most of the military and police forces. Oh God – They've just broken into our station – What the hell..."

The signal went silent. All we heard was static. A moment later, we heard explosions that shook the ground. Fear and panic filled the basement.

"What the hell was that?" asked Marc.

"That did not sound good," I said, feeling uneasy.

"Oh, my God – What's going on?" said Laura, who was very frightened.

"Everyone, find a hiding place now," I ordered.

"Duck and cover," Evan added.

We all ran into Marc's office and hid under his desk. Evan put a vertical file cabinet in front of the door and secured it there. Laura, Rebekah, Marc, and Jason huddled really close together. I could see the fear in all of their faces. A couple of minutes later, we heard the sound of the front door being kicked open. Heavy footsteps echoed upstairs. We also heard animal-like grunting and growling sounds. Marc's mom and dad yelled at the intruders while being dragged out of the house. Thankfully, whatever was up there forgot to check the basement.

The upstairs went silent. Screams and gunfire can be heard outside. We stayed low until the bedlam ceased.

"Something took mom and dad," said Laura.

"We're gonna die, we're gonna die," said Jason, hyperventilating.

"Shh," I said.

"I'm so scared right now," said Rebekah, starting to cry a bit.

"Hang in there, everyone. We're going to get through this – We have to be strong," I said.

"Man, this is some scary stuff. What the hell is going on out there?" asked Evan.

"Whatever it is, I don't want to know," said Marc.

An hour had passed and the amount of activity outside diminished. Explosions discontinued, screams silenced, and any aggressors seemed to have left the area. We waited another fifteen minutes before doing anything. I looked around at everyone and saw uncertainty, sadness, and fear in their eyes.

"Is it safe?" asked Jason.

"I think so," I replied.

We emerged from under Marc's desk. Evan moved the vertical file away and I carefully opened the door. The two windows in the basement were covered up by dirt. All of us proceeded to the couch, sat down, and tried to process what had just happened.

"Oh, my God, what just happened?" asked Rebekah.

"Was that the end of the world?" asked Jason.

"I don't like the look of this. Explosions, screams, monstrous sounds – Something is not right," said Chris.

"We should investigate," said Bill.

"Are you insane? I'm staying down here," exclaimed Jason.

"Yeah, I'm not investigating – I'm staying put," said Rebekah.

"Me, too," said Laura.

It was no surprise to see everyone reluctant. To be stuck in the basement with very little resources, we would not last long. With the food and water on reserve, it'll hold us for three days, if we're lucky. Our only option was to venture out. I volunteered to check and see if the coast was clear.

"Guys, I'm going to go up there and see if the coast is clear. We can't stay in this basement forever. We need to know what happened so we can figure out what to do next."

"Alan, you realize that some hostile forces just barged their way into Marc's house. We don't even know if some are silently holding a position somewhere up there," said Chris.

"I am quite aware of that, Chris. That's why I'm willing to go and check it out so you guys don't have to face any unfortunate consequences."

"Al, wait. I'll go with you. Evan, guard the stairway. In case anything goes wrong, you protect everyone else," said Marc.

"Got it," Evan replied.

Marc and I slowly climbed the stairs to the door. We carefully avoided any movement causing the stairs to creak or squeak. As I approached the door, I moved my hand slowly to the knob. I looked back at Marc and could tell he was extremely nervous. I took a deep breath and turned the knob slowly. Putting pressure on the door, I could feel my heart beating faster. I opened the door slowly, keeping my ears perked for any sounds of something in the house.

"Is it clear?" asked Marc.

"So far, it is. Your house is all messed up but no life forms are present," I replied

It appeared to be safe to proceed. Marc and I carefully emerged from the basement and got ready to explore. The dining room was obliterated – the table split in half, chairs broken, cabinets tipped over, and the sliding door, leading to the backyard, smashed. An orange haze can be seen outside – a lot of dust and smoke drifted in the air. A sense of dread overwhelmed me.

"Alright, let's see if we can figure out what happened here," I said.

"Hopefully, there are some items salvageable in my house. Wait, there is something in my room I need to make sure wasn't destroyed," said Marc.

"What is it?"

"It's this special device I made for the computer. It can actually tap into other electronic devices via two wire cables."

"Be careful, Marc. I'll standby down here."

Marc proceeded up the stairs to his room. After he made his way there, I heard him gasp. Something must have startled him. I made my way upstairs and saw what freaked him out. His room had this big hole in the wall looking out onto his backyard. Scratch marks covered the walls and his room lay in ruin.

Marc shrieked, "My room. What the hell did this? Where's my device?"

He proceeded to look for it within the rubble. In the meantime, I decided to check the other rooms to see if I could figure out what happened. With many scratch marks on the walls, it looked like lions or tigers ran through the entire house. I reported back to Marc to check on him.

"Did you find it?" I asked.

Marc dug a little deeper and came across his device.

"Yes – Thank goodness I found it. Alright, let's head back down to let everyone know it's safe to come out."

"Marc, I looked around the rest of the upstairs but still I can't figure out what the hell happened here. The big hole in your wall I can't really put my finger on but the scratch marks, busted down doors, and broken windows, I think something vicious barged its way into your house."

"What could possibly make scratch marks on the wall? Did a stampede of bears run through here?"

"I don't think it's that. Your parents were struggling with something. It's like someone or something was dragging them out using force. Also, you could hear the intruders' thumping footsteps."

"Good point. Let's head back down and let everyone know it's safe. We'll discuss further in the den."

We went back down to the basement to inform everyone it was safe to come out. Chris, Bill, Evan, Laura, Jason, and Rebekah proceeded to the family room. Someone screamed and it wasn't the girls.

"Jason, my goodness, do you really have to scream like that?" asked Marc.

"There are dead people lying in the street," exclaimed Jason.

"Oh, my God," Rebekah shrieked.

A few people lay dead on the street. Mangled cars and tons of property damage completed the morbid scene.

"Oh, God – This can't be real..." said Laura, covering her mouth in shock.

"Holy crap," said Evan.

"This is disturbing – What the hell happened here? I can't believe I'm actually seeing this," said Chris.

Looking at the horrible sight, I felt like my whole world came crashing down on me. Inside, I felt like I lost another chunk of my life. Another round of emotional pain to deal with – another Hell to endure.

"I wonder what did all that," I said.

"Maybe we should check it out," said Bill.

"Are you crazy? It's too dangerous – Who knows if something could still be out there," exclaimed Jason.

"J, calm down. Bill is right in a way. We really should investigate the area. We don't have to go far from the house but still we need answers," I said.

"I think we should stay inside – I know for sure it's safer here," said Rebekah.

"By the looks of this situation, I say we aren't safe anywhere," said Evan.

"Okay, we aren't getting anywhere just by having contradicting thoughts of the situation. Some of us are saying investigate and some say not to. So, what will it be?" I asked.

"If we investigate the area, we may figure out whom or what invaded. Once we know that, we can figure a way around this. Alan even mentioned that earlier," said Bill.

"Anyway, it'll only be four of us. Two will head in one direction while the other two go the opposite," I said.

"Okay, so, what's your idea?" asked Marc.

"Alright, you and I will go west. Chris and Bill, you two will go east. Evan, you will guard the door and protect everyone else."

"I'll get my video camera. I would like to get some footage while we explore," said Bill.

"Before we go, let me get my tools," said Marc.

Marc got two medium-sized pipe wrenches out from his toolbox and gave one to Chris. My friends and I got ready to embark on a dangerous exploration into the unknown. We had no idea what we would face but we had to do it. It's one step for man, one giant leap into Hell.

"Are you guys ready?" I asked.

"Yep," they all replied.

"Good luck guys – I'll defend the base," said Evan.

We stepped outside and I could smell the horrible odor of burning materials and the rotting dead. It really felt like stepping into Hell. I looked back at my friends and I can see how uneasy they were. Marc and I went our direction while Chris and Bill went their direction.

Marc and I walked along the sidewalk and carefully moved our way around debris and a couple of bodies. He went over to one of the dead bodies and examined the wounds.

"Alan, take a look at this. Look at these wounds. It looks like an animal attacked this person."

"Fascinating – If you look at the left arm, it looks like something took a chunk out of him."

"Gross, man – I really can't tell what happened to these people. There's definitely no stab or gunshot wounds – Nothing like an attack from human opposition."

"Well Marc, I think I found a clue to what may have hit here – Look at this footprint."

I pointed to the footprint. It's shaped similar to a human's but slightly larger. At the end of the print, near the toes, there seemed to be the presence of talons.

"Oh, my God – Look at the size of this. This is just a tad larger than Evan's foot – And look, talons near the toes. What the hell made this print?" asked Marc.

"I know for sure a human didn't leave that print."

"Are you saying we may have been invaded by humanoid creatures?"

"Maybe, or some guy needs to cut his toenails."

While Marc and I pondered about the print, I started hearing an odd sound coming from around the neighbor's house. It sounded like a pack of wolves feasting on a kill.

"Marc, do you hear that sound?"

"Yeah…"

"It's coming from behind your neighbor's house."

"I don't think it's a wise idea to check it out."

"It may give us more answers to what is going on around here."

"Okay, but I really have a bad feeling about this."

Marc and I approached the house quietly. We were flat up against the siding. I prepared myself to take a look. Something unpleasant waited around the corner. Taking a deep breath, I took a quick peek. To my amazement, I saw something I would never imagine myself seeing in my lifetime. There stood a dark-green, six-and-a-half feet tall, lizard man, digging into a thawed steak he pulled out of an outdoor fridge. Shocked by this discovery, I came back around for cover.

"What is it?" asked Marc.

"You would not believe me if I told you. Take a look for yourself," I replied.

Marc took a quick glance and came back around after the first second he saw the lizard man. I looked at him and saw a shocked expression on his face. He was definitely scared stiff.

"Let's get the hell out of here," said Marc.

Marc and I fled the scene. The sight of the lizard man caused Marc to shake frantically.

"Was that a lizard man?" asked Marc.

"Indeed it is," I replied.

"Holy crap."

"Shh – Keep it down, man. You'll blow our cover. We can't take any chances of having that lizard man following us back."

"Dammit, I should've thought of that. Let's head back and let everyone know."

"I wonder if Chris and Bill found anything interesting."

Marc and I retreated back to his house and met up with Chris and Bill. We walked over to Evan and briefly discussed our findings.

"So, did you guys find anything interesting?" asked Evan.

"Hell yeah – We found something that pretty much explains what happened here," replied Marc.

"We found something pretty interesting as well. Bill recorded it on his camera," said Chris.

"What did you and Al find?" asked Bill.

"Well, we found something that was quite a shock to us, right Alan?"

"Indeed, Marc. We found a lizard man eating behind the neighbor's house."

"A lizard man? Are you for real, homes? What's he eating?" asked Evan.

"That reptilian humanoid was eating some stuff from my neighbor's outdoor fridge," said Marc.

"You think that was freaky, Bill and I found something just as whacky as that," said Chris.

"I'll show you guys – I have it on film," said Bill.

He got the camera ready to preview the footage. We all gathered around to see it. To our surprise, Chris and Bill came across a gargoyle rummaging through someone's trash can. What we knew as myths and legends now came to life before our very eyes.

"This is amazing. You two spotted an actual gargoyle. Excellent work," I said.

"Thank you, Mister Alan," said Bill.

"What's really fascinating is that these are the creatures I write about in my stories. It's like fantasy has become real," I said.

"It does seem that way. I wonder if other legendary beasts have come to life," said Chris.

"Let's hope there's nothing too big. I don't think we can handle creatures like a dragon or something," said Evan.

"Yeah, let's hope not. Let's get back inside and discuss this with the others," said Marc.

While heading in, I heard movement to the left of me, fifty feet away from my position. I looked for a moment and I noticed a lizard-like tail moving behind a bush. In the back of my mind, I was thinking the lizard man spotted us. Hopefully, he would just leave us alone. Knowing him, he'd want to get his claws on every bit of human meat.

"What's up, Al?" asked Marc.

"Marc, I could've sworn I saw something move over by those bushes."

"What did you see?"

"I thought I saw a tail vanishing into the shrubbery like something just quickly hid itself."

"Let's get inside and secure the doors. I don't want to take any chances."

We went inside feeling uneasy. I could sense that lizard man drawing closer to the house, waiting for the right moment to attack us. Marc closed the door and moved a cabinet in front of it. We all proceeded to the den to discuss our findings.

DISCUSSION
4

I shut the door and everyone sat down. Evan helped move some things out of the way and positioned the coffee table in front of the door as a precaution. I stood up at the front of the room and got ready to speak.

"Okay everyone, after searching the perimeter for clues, Marc, myself, Chris, and Bill came across shocking evidence," I started.

"Alan and I found a lizard man," said Marc.

"You found what?" Rebekah asked nervously.

"A lizard man?" asked Laura.

"You're joking – Monsters don't exist," said Jason.

"Bill has some footage of another being that was hanging around here," said Chris.

Everyone gathered around to see the footage on Bill's camera. Once Rebekah, Laura, and Jason saw the video of the gargoyle, their jaws dropped.

"You guys were right," said Jason.

"Oh my God, oh my God, oh my God," Rebekah repeated.

"I hope mom and dad weren't eaten by these monsters," said Laura.

"I sure hope not, sis," said Marc.

"So, what's the plan?" asked Evan.

"Okay, what we need to do is figure out what we can do to get through this situation…" I started.

"Exactly – Let's see how we can live the rest of our lives not messing with those monsters. So, what can we do for food, shelter..." said Jason, interrupting me.

"Hold on one sec, Jason. There is no way in hell we can survive with those things walking around. Even if we found another location, they would be able to sniff us out eventually," said Chris.

"I definitely agree with you, Chris. These beings look like they are good hunters and I bet they could smell a human a mile away," said Marc.

"I don't want those creatures touching me or eating me or anything of that sort – Eww." said Rebekah.

"Listen, we have to find out what brought these creatures here and end the nightmare. Yes, I'm a little uneasy about doing it but we have no choice," I said.

"Alan, it'll be too risky. We're better off staying here," said Jason.

All around the room, I saw reluctance. I could understand my proposition was dangerous. If these creatures wanted a piece of us, they're going to have to fight me to get to my friends – I wasn't going to go down without a fight. I had to think of something to motivate them to help save our friends, family, and any civilians remaining.

"You know, I once read a quote on a video game web site that caught my eye," I started to say, "Evil wins when good people do nothing. Do you guys want evil to win and threaten our freedom?

Do you feel it is okay for evil to violate justice? Do you think it is okay to live in fear?" I paused for a moment, looking around the room. My friends focused their attention on me with a stoic expression. I continued,

"How about you all push that fear aside and show this evil we are not afraid. Sure, I'm kind of daunted by this situation, but I'm not going to let fear hold me back. The human race is in trouble and we can't just sit here and do nothing. Our friends and family are in danger, for crying out loud," I paused again, my friends looking at each other, thinking about the words I had said.

"A year ago, I came home and found my father dying on the floor. I didn't back down - I went and I did all I can do to help him. We must do what is right for the greater good. Apparently, the police and military failed to keep these creatures back and many of them probably died. We have to do something. Will you help me?" I finished.

The room was silent. I looked around and then Jason spoke up,

"Alan, those games are really rotting your mind. Sitting ducks or not, we're still dead. We'll be lunch meat for those monsters within a few days. We're dead one way or another."

"Hold on a sec, J. Yes, it does sound like a long shot but I see no other way. It sounds like a crazy idea, and it is, but if we don't do anything, our friends and family will surely perish. Chris was definitely right that these beings would probably sniff us out and get us easily. If we stay here, we will get killed by these… things. However, we still might get killed even if we do leave here but our chances for survival would be better than being sitting ducks. I say let's do it. Let's go out and save everyone," said Marc.

"I'm with you guys. Time to show these monsters we ain't goin' down without a fight," said Evan.

"Yeah, another clichéd story about a group of teens saving the world," said Bill, with excitement.

"Wait a minute. How are we going to defeat these creatures if we're going to fight them?" asked Jason.

"With weaponry, of course," I replied.

"And where are we going to get these weapons?" he asked again.

"There's an arms shop near the University. They should have the necessary equipment we need," said Chris.

"Also, we can take a trip over to the police station and get more equipment," Evan added.

"Excellent idea – Alright, let's make a list of supplies we need to get," I said.

"I'll take care of that," said Chris.

Jason still had a lot of misgivings over my plan but he went along with it. I sensed Rebekah and Laura had doubts, too, but I know with our teamwork, we all would be fine. Everyone else, I could sense, had a rush of confidence. Chris finished up the list of items needed and Marc looked it over.

"It's a little dark in here. Can I open the blinds a little?" asked Rebekah.

"Sure, but just a little," I replied.

Rebekah opened the blinds and screamed. We looked towards the window and saw the lizard man peeking in. He growled and left some fog on the window from his breath. Next, he left and ran across the backyard in the direction of the sliding door in the dining room.

"That was the lizard man?" shrieked Laura.

"Oh, my God," exclaimed Rebekah.

"We're dead, we're dead..." Jason repeated.

"Evan and Chris, hold the door shut. Everyone else, go out the window and head straight to the van," I ordered.

"Al, I'll secure the van and get it up and running," said Marc, grabbing his computer device.

"Roger that," I acknowledged.

Everyone escaped through the window while the three of us held the door shut. We heard the lizard man running toward the door and then ramming it, roaring and scratching aggressively. For a moment, we thought he would bash the door down even though the three of us held it closed with the coffee table.

"Chris and Al, you guys go. I'll handle this guy," ordered Evan.

"Are you sure Evan?" I asked.

"Just go – I'll buy you guys some time."

Chris and I exited through the window. I told Chris to meet up with the rest and let them know I'll catch up while I wait for Evan. I needed everyone alive in order to proceed with the mission. Peeking through the window, I saw the lizard man clawing his way through the door. Evan quickly grabbed an ottoman nearby and secured it next to the coffee table. He ran to the window.

"Al, what are you still doing here?"

"Hey, I wasn't going to let my buddy get eaten by a lizard man."

"Let's roll."

As Evan and I hopped over the fence to the front yard, we heard the lizard man bust down the door and roared. We ran to the van. Thankfully, we all made it unscathed. Just as Marc put the van in gear, another lizard man dropped down. He landed on the hood and roared at us. He punched the windshield causing it to crack a little. Marc sped off in reverse, throwing the lizard man off as he swung the vehicle left.

"Pedal to the metal, Marc," I ordered.

Marc put the van in drive and floored it.

"That was freaky," said Rebekah, trying to catch her breath.

"Where the hell did they come from?" asked Marc.

"Looks like we've got plenty of humanoid creatures," said Bill.

"Sure seems that way," I added.

"I'm scared, guys. These creatures are freaking me out," said Laura.

"Don't worry – If a monster comes after you, I'll pop a cap on his ass," said Evan.

"From this point forward, guys, we are not safe," I said.

We proceeded in the direction of the arms shop. I know Evan can beat down bad guys but ones with razor-sharp claws and teeth, I doubt he would have a chance. Usually, I'm not one who condones violence of any sort but, based on our circumstance, we needed substantial weaponry to defend ourselves. In addition, we would need some useful equipment like armor and medical supplies. Thankfully, Marc had a jumbo medkit in the backseat. It may be enough for minor injuries but if several of us take critical damage during an encounter, there wouldn't be enough supplies to treat serious injuries.

Alan J. Duin

Our adventure started out a bit rough - who knew what we were in for next. I know for sure I didn't set the difficulty setting to our situation and I can safely say it wasn't on easy. It felt more like medium to me, especially for level one. After getting a taste of what it's like to run from danger, I felt it's going to get harder later on – perhaps even nightmarish.

LOCK N' LOAD
5

Chris directed Marc in the direction of the arms shop. While riding down Hempstead Turnpike, we could see the amount of destruction these creatures did to Levittown. It was depressing to see our once beautiful town had been destroyed.

We came across more destruction while approaching East Meadow and Garden City. Destroyed military units could be seen down the road. Hummers, soldier transports, and even a couple of helicopters lie in ruin. The dead, too, littered the ground. We were knee-deep in Hell.

"Alan, what are we going to do after we arm up?" asked Bill.

"After we lock and load, we will head to the Hicksville department store to pick up tools and other supplies," I replied.

"What kind of supplies are you thinking of?" asked Bill.

"We could pick up stuff from the hardware department to help us construct armor and devices. Also, some stuff in that department may have items that could be used as weapons."

"What are we doing after that?"

"Next we will head to the police station to get some Kevlar vests and some EMT medical equipment. Afterwards, we will locate Mike and Charles, God willing, they are still safe in their homes."

"I hope Mike's alright – I hope he was able to find cover," said Chris.

"Yeah, I hope so, too. We need him for navigation," Bill added.

As we approached our destination, a few military vehicles lie decimated – some still on fire. Marc stopped the van and I opened the side door.

"Alright – Evan, Jason, and Laura, stay here and guard the van," I ordered.

"Roger that," Evan acknowledged.

"As for me, Marc, Chris, Bill, and Rebekah, we will go inside."

We exited the van and looked at the destruction before us. One of the Hummers near the store was in fair condition. We decided to go over to it and see if we could find anything salvageable. Rebekah decided to hold a spot near the van. She felt uneasy investigating the vehicle – couldn't blame her.

"I'm going to look inside," said Marc.

He opened the driver side door and out came a dead soldier's body. Marc gasped at the horrible sight and the rest of us cringed.

"I'm going to check the trunk," I said.

I went around back and found the trunk already unlocked. Opening it, I found a mother lode of arsenal and equipment. There was an M-16, an M249 SAW, two MP5K's, three regular MP5's, a P-90, and an AK-47. In addition, I found a generous amount of ammo for these weapons. Next, I found flashlights, a few walkie-talkies, and some grenades.

"Guys, I found a generous amount of firepower in here," I said.

"Thank goodness these weapons survived the attack," said Chris.

"Would this cover us or do we need some more guns?" asked Bill.

"We may need more. Hang on, I have an idea," I replied.

I needed someone to gather all the stuff in the trunk and put it neatly in the back of the van. There's only one man who can do it.

"Yo, Evan," I called out.

"Yo," he replied.

"Can you come over here for a second?"

Evan came over and looked inside the trunk. He was amazed at the amount of weaponry we found.

"Whoa, you hit the jackpot, man," he said.

"Evan, would you be kind enough to load these weapons into the back of the van? Also, take as much ammo as you can – We are going to need it."

"You got it, Al."

"For the rest of us, let us proceed in to the store and find some bonus weaponry and ammo," I said.

The five of us walked up to the store and went in. To our surprise, a lot of weapons were gone. However, a suitable amount remained. I grabbed a 12-gauge pump-action shotgun on the wall and put it on the counter. Two other shotguns caught my eye – a pump-action Mossberg 500 with a pistol grip and a double barrel, break-action, shotgun with a sawed down barrel stock. I, too, obtained five boxes of shells.

Marc grabbed a few pistols. He took two Berettas, a couple of Colt 1911's, and two Glocks. In addition, he grabbed thirty clips – ten for each pistol type. He placed them on the counter next to the shotguns.

Chris and Bill searched through the store to locate anything else we could use. Rebekah obtained a six-shooter with a box of ammo and put it on the counter with the rest. Chris and Bill came back with ammo pouches, a shell belt, and a large backpack. Hopefully, this would be enough.

"Monsters check in," started Marc while loading a clip into a Glock.

I pumped the shotgun and said, "They don't check out."

"Do we have everything?" asked Chris.

Bill answered, "I think we have everything."

We put the ammo and pistols into the backpack and carried the shotguns separately. As we exited the store, Evan had just finished loading the van. He signaled us to come over to him.

"Hey guys, guess what I found?"

Evan pulled out of the Hummer something I didn't see in there. It was the minigun – a heavy-weight Gatling gun capable of turning a target into Swiss cheese.

"Take a look at this bad boy."

"Wow Evan, where was that in the trunk?" I asked.

"It was in this box way in the back. Pretty cool gun, eh?"

"This would definitely make those monsters run," said Chris.

"Damn straight, homie."

Evan attempted to put the minigun in the trunk area. Unfortunately, it couldn't fit. He then tried the back seat where it did fit nice and comfortably along with the chain of six thousand rounds. Before we could go, a wounded soldier signaled us. Marc grabbed the med kit and ran over to him. The soldier had serious injuries. His condition did not look good. Rubble had crushed his right leg while a metal piece protruding from a concrete wall penetrated his left leg, impaling it. His torso appeared to have a couple of gashes from razor-sharp claws. We can see this soldier had lost a considerable amount of blood by looking at the stained asphalt under him.

"Hey..." called the soldier.

"Sir, what happened?" asked Marc.

"These creatures came out of nowhere. My team had no chance..."

"Hang on, I'll bandage some of those wounds," said Marc.

"It's not worth it. I'm a dead man anyway. Here, take my knife – You may need it. Everybody's dead here. The human race is in trouble – We have failed – You're all we have left. Find out who did this."

"We will sir – Always faithful," I said while saluting.

"Be careful – There are weapons in the Hummer. You can use those to defend yourselves. Good luck and God's speed."

The soldier began fading, his life slowly slipping away. Eventually, he took his last breath and was gone.

"Let's go, guys, we got work to do," said Evan.

"Let's move out," I ordered.

    We all reported back to the van and got ready to head to the Hicksville department store. Once there, I felt we may encounter a combat situation. We might face something more horrible – perhaps hordes of creatures or maybe something bigger and stronger. Since our scenario felt like the video games I played, we have yet to encounter stronger enemies – maybe even bosses. Either way, we must stay together and work as a team to survive.

ALIENS AND DEMONS
6

Marc drove down Hempstead Turnpike and turned onto Jordan Avenue, taking it to Hicksville near the mall. He proceeded down the road doing his best to get around debris. As we entered the store parking lot, wrecked cars littered the place.

"Find any parking spots?" asked Marc, sarcastically.

"Marc, hold a position near the entrance," I ordered.

He drove up to the curb near the south entrance. I knew this store had some useful stuff the last time I went. Hopefully, the inside wasn't too beat up from the attack.

"So, what's the plan?" asked Evan.

"Okay, here is who will be going in. It will be Marc, myself, Evan, and Rebekah," I replied.

"Me? Why me?" asked Rebekah, aggressively.

"I need at least three other people, Beka. Two with strength and one science-tech guy," I explained.

"Fine, but I don't feel good about going in there."

"Scared, Beka?" teased Marc.

"Quit it, Marc. Keep it up and I'll take that gun and shove it up your..."

"Guys, calm down," I interrupted, "Now let us get ready to head inside."

The four of us exited the van and went to the back. I decided to use the Mossberg 500 just in case we came across heavy combat. Marc and Evan each took an MP5 and a few mags. Lastly, Rebekah took a Beretta and a couple of clips – she even took the knife the soldier gave us, just in case. I loaded the eight shells into the shotgun and took some extra ammo. After loading up, I went over to the passenger side of the van to talk to Chris.

"Alan, how long do you want us to wait until we should come in after you?"

"I'd say at least twenty minutes. Hopefully, we shouldn't run into any problems," I replied.

"Okay."

"Good luck, guys," said Bill.

"Thank you, Bill," I replied.

"Be careful in there – Don't get killed," said Chris.

"We'll try and be careful," said Marc.

"Good luck, guys," said Laura.

"Yeah – Be careful in there," Jason added.

Marc grabbed a couple of flashlights and took a walkie-talkie. Just in case we needed back up, we would be able to contact Chris. We approached the building entrance and got ready. It appeared to be dark inside.

"Okay, I'll enter first – Evan, you follow behind me – Rebekah, you stay behind your brother, and Marc, you'll cover the rear."

"Why do I have to be behind my brother? I don't want to have to smell his farts," said Rebekah.

"Mmm… fartville coming your way," said Evan.

"Eww – You're so gross, Evan," said Rebekah.

"Guys, can we stick to the mission?" I asked, with a serious tone.

I opened the door. As we entered, only a few lights were lit - some of them flickered. We looked around to see what happened and it appeared the invaders barged into the store to carry out their deed. The store was quiet... way too quiet.

"Man, it's creepy in here," said Marc.

"I don't like the look of this at all," said Evan.

"Can we go back?" asked Rebekah.

As we were walking along, the sound of glass breaking in the distance followed by a sound of breath echoed. My eyes continuously darted left and right – my heartbeat was a little faster – fear flowed through me. We had no idea what made the sound. I hoped we didn't have to come across it.

"What was that?" asked Rebekah while trembling.

"There's *something* here," said Evan.

"The question is what," Marc added.

"Let's proceed onward. Keep your eyes peeled," I said.

We walked further down past the jewelry counter, near the winter apparel section. Despite it wasn't winter anymore, the store had a clearance sale, making room for spring and summer. I went over to the vests and took a red one.

"Why are we stopping here?" asked Rebekah.

"These may provide some protection. It may lessen the blow from an attack."

My friends joined in taking vests for themselves and for the rest of our friends. After our "end-of-the-world" shopping spree, Rebekah grabbed a large gym bag lying on the floor and put all the vests in there.

"Okay, let's get to the hardware department, get what we need, and get out of here," I said.

Approaching the escalators, we saw something extremely weird. A wall composed of some kind of strange material blocked our path.

"What the hell?" I said, sounding confused.

"Eww, looks gross," said Rebekah.

"Let me get a closer look at it," said Marc.

Carefully approaching the anomalous wall, he analyzed it. He then picked up a hanger on the floor and poked it gently.

"Guys, this wall here is composed of mucus and other tissues I've never seen before."

"Mucus? What in Sam hell could have made a whole wall out of mucus and other organic materials?" I questioned.

"Either way, this is gross," said Rebekah.

"Do you want me to cut through it?" asked Evan.

"Not yet – We don't know what would happen if we puncture it," I said.

While thinking about what to do, the lights near the escalator flickered. It flashed on and revealed something disturbing. There was an extension to the mucus wall but within it were people locked in some kind of sack. It felt like science fiction came to life. Something told me we were going to encounter some odd beings.

"Holy cow," said Evan.

"Oh, my god," said Rebekah while covering her mouth.

"I wonder what kind of life forms did this," I said.

After our surprise, we started hearing a sound from behind a cash register counter. I was about to investigate until a creature came up over the counter and hissed at us. The creature had blue skin with a purple midsection. It had sharp teeth, an elongated head, and green glowing eyes with a slit pupil. It sat atop the counter poised to attack. Within a second, the creature lunged towards us. Evan knocked it off course. He wrestled with the creature and kicked it in the groin, temporarily stunning it, and punched it several times until it was knocked out cold.

"Yeah, you like that blue boy? Too easy," said Evan, cracking his knuckles.

Marc went over to examine the creature. It had green blood

bleeding from its mouth.

"By looking at this creature's tissues and the fact that it has neon green blood, I'd say this is an alien. Seriously, this bodily tissue is very different from earth-born organisms. I don't think it's even carbon-based."

"Damn, man. Now we have to deal with aliens. Well, at least they were easy to beat," said Evan.

"Since this organism has insect-like behavior, there are bound to be plenty more – Maybe even a higher power exists," I said.

"There are more of them?" questioned Rebekah.

"Possibly…" I started to say then hearing a loud sound, "…and maybe a king or queen."

The sound echoed from the hardware department on the lower level. It sounded like a large life form with a mechanical-like roar. Something big, bad, and ugly was coming – well, the bad and the ugly are guaranteed.

"That did not sound good," said Marc.

"We should go," said Rebekah.

At the bottom of the escalators, a man ran up and jumped towards the railing, bordering the upstairs. The man had some trouble but managed to get over. As soon as he did, we saw something that made us stare in awe. This large creature jumped up onto the escalator and jumped towards the railing, knocking it down. The creature looked like a mix of the smaller alien but this time with a centaur-like appearance. It had four arms – two regular and two with large talons at the end. In addition, it had six eyes and some feminine features.

The creature grabbed the man and dragged him back down to the hardware department. We heard the creature screech and then heard the man scream in agony followed by a lot of disgusting gory sounds. For a moment, it went silent. My blood went cold from witnessing the horror. What we saw left us frozen with fear. We had to get out of there and get out of there now.

"Holy crap – What the hell was that thing?" asked Evan, frantically.

"I think it's time to abort the objective – Retreat," I ordered.

As we were about to leave, the creature jumped up from the lower level and made its way to the main floor. This behemoth stood in front of us ready to slaughter its next prey. I knew this creature was the queen. She stood about eight feet tall and probably six to eight feet in length. The queen roared at us with a bloodied mouth. Her eyes looked menacing. She let out a screech summoning some alien minions and backed off to let them come after us. Hostiles dropped down from the ceiling and surrounded us. If we took down the ones blocking the path to the exit, we'd have a chance.

"What do we do?" asked Rebekah, panicking.

"Let me handle these freaks," said Evan.

"Wait, we'll do a charging run," I said.

"I have a bad feeling about that," said Rebekah.

"Guys, they're getting closer," exclaimed Marc.

"On three – One, two, three," I said.

We did a charging run towards the aliens and fired our weapons at them, blasting them into green sludge as we made our way through. The queen came after us and caught up fast. She went back down to the lower level and jumped up through the floor in front of us, giving a loud roar. We ran back towards the escalators and encountered a few more alien minions. Fortunately, Evan took them down with ease. The queen slowly approached us, exposing her sharp teeth with saliva dripping down from them. We knew she wanted a full course meal but I wasn't going to let her put us on the menu.

"Any ideas?" asked Marc.

"Let me handle this – Hoowaaaaaaaa…" shouted Evan.

Evan lunged towards the queen with his MP5 firing. She smacked him to the side and he flew into a display wall.

"Evan," shouted Rebekah.

Marc went in for a closer shot but while doing so, the queen went onto her hind legs and kicked him with her frontal legs, knocking him back far.

"That hurt," said Marc while in pain.

"What do we do?" asked Rebekah.

"Circle behind her," I ordered.

"Say what?" she asked again.

"Just go – Trust me," I ordered.

    I loaded extra shells into the shotgun and prepared for one hell of a fight. The queen made a few attempts to scratch me but I strafed out of the way and unloaded some firepower on her. I backed off to reload. Marc started to fire at the queen taking her attention away from me. She was closing in on him and then suddenly, Evan jumped onto her back to distract her.

"Gotcha, bitch," exclaimed Evan.

    The queen struggled to get Evan off her back. She managed to grab him and bring him around to her front. She roared in Evan's face. Certainly, he had something to say in reply.

"God damn, get a mint, 'cause yo breath stinks."

    The queen looked like she wanted to take a bite out of him. Marc's gun was jammed and I couldn't use the shotgun because the spread would hit Evan. Rebekah, being the only other person who could do something, whipped out the knife, came behind the queen, and stabbed her butt. She spun around to face Rebekah and tossed Evan at her. Both were knocked to the floor.

"Evan and Beka are down – What now?" asked Marc.

"Marc, I'm going to look for something better to take down this beast."

"What do you have in mind?"

"Something in the hardware department. I need you to hold her off until I get back – I won't be long."

"You want me to hold her off?"

"You can do it, Marc. Take Evan's MP5 and keep her busy."

"Oh, crud."

I quickly ran off to the escalators. I took a hanger rack and used it to puncture the mucus wall. I went down to the lower level to look for a motorized tool. While searching for it, I could hear Marc's status with the queen.

"You don't want to eat me. Look, I'm short and uh... not really fat," said Marc.

"You seem very delectable, human. Don't worry – It'll all be over soon," said the queen.

"You can talk?"

"Yes, I can. Now prepare to meet your doom..."

Quickly grabbing what I was looking for, I found a chainsaw with just enough fuel in it. I ran back up before Marc became lunch meat. Thankfully, I returned in time. The queen was closing in on him. I whistled loudly and got her attention.

"Yo, queeny," I said while pulling on the pull cord of the chainsaw, "Let's go."

"Fear me, human."

My strategy was to slice off her talon arms. It might make it easier to take her down. The queen started to come at me and I ducked down under her first attack. She swung her right talon arm and I sliced through it. Screaming in pain, she turned to me aggressively.

"I'll bite your head off for that," the queen yelled.

"Let's rock."

The queen came at me again and I did the same strategy as before – this time the left was sliced off. She screamed in pain.

"What foul weapon are you holding?" the queen asked aggressively.

"You see this? This is a chainsaw – The best tool any man can have not only to cut wood but also slice down alien scum like you."

"You shall pay for your insolence."

"Come on," I exclaimed.

She came towards me and slashed my left arm causing me to drop the chainsaw. The damage I took was painful but I wasn't going down due to a few cuts. I ran over to where I left the shotgun and grabbed it just in time – she was *really* close.

"Die human – I'll swallow your head," she yelled.

"Swallow this," I shouted.

I took my shotgun and fired every shot I had. Every blast knocked her back. One, two three – the queen screeched in pain – four, five, six – the queen was weakening – seven and eight – the queen fell to the ground. I loaded some extra shells in my gun and walked carefully over to her. The queen looked up at me with the remaining strength she had.

"You're afraid, little human. I can see it in you – The fear devouring you."

"I am not afraid of you – I will not let fear hold me back – Fear can be conquered and so can you."

She then breathed her last breath and died. The queen has been defeated and my friends were safe... for now. Marc came over to me in disbelief.

"Alan, that was bad-ass. Excellent work, buddy. Let me wrap some gauze around your arms – she got you pretty bad," said Marc.

"Thanks, Marc. First, let's go check on Evan and Rebekah."

Marc and I rushed over to them. Thankfully, they were okay – they only suffered minor injuries. Marc took out a small stimpack and proceeded to wrap my arms in gauze.

"Man, I'm sore from that," said Evan.

"Me, too," Rebekah added.

Before we left, I noticed a toolbox on the floor near one of the display tables. I went over and got it – I gave it to Marc to hold. It wasn't the main thing we came for, however, it is still useful. Rebekah got the bag of vests and we walked towards the exit.

"Okay guys, let's pack it in and get out of here," I said.

We made our way outside and went over to the van. Everybody was happy to see us come out.

"Finally – What took you so long? I was about to send in Bill and Jason," said Chris.

"Long story, but I'll tell you later," I replied.

"What is that green stuff all over you?" asked Chris.

"He'll explain later," replied Marc.

"By the way, Bill and I got some scrap metal from the busted cars out here. Some of the pieces can be used as armor. You see, we have some that look like shoulder pads, knee pads, and shin guards," said Chris.

"Well done. When we arrive back at my house, we'll sort them out and get them ready to be armor pieces."

"Sounds like a plan," said Chris.

"Cool," Bill added.

Marc put the van in gear and sped off to the police station. Since he bypassed areas where the traffic lights would be, it took us ten minutes to get there. As we approached the station, we can already see something horrible. Outside, we saw dehydrated-looking corpses. I opened the left sliding door and got ready to give the briefing.

"Okay guys, it'll be me, Marc, Chris, and Bill. We need to look for bonus equipment and, if possible, extra weaponry."

I told Evan to defend the van while we're inside. The four of us loaded up and got ready to explore the station. Aside from the weird looking corpses in front, the plants around the building, too, had an odd appearance. Something seemed ominous but we needed to get the extra equipment, especially the EMT medical packs.

Entering the station, we noticed an eerie red hue illuminating the lobby and the smell of something foul within the air. We looked to our right and saw jet-black candles floating in mid-air down a hallway. Looking to our left, we saw a few dead bodies down the other hall.

"This is friggin' weird," said Marc.

"What's the plan?" asked Bill.

"We'll split up like before. Marc and I will go down the hallway with a few dead people. You and Chris will go down the hallway with those ominous floating candles."

"Okay, so, we just need to look for a supply room with the necessary equipment, right?" asked Chris.

"Precisely – If you find anything, report in," I replied.

Marc and I proceeded down the hallway with dead bodies. As we passed by some doors, we noticed the ones with the blurred windows had blood on them. This place gave off a bad vibe – something evil was here. We continued further down and came to a corner. I carefully looked around it to make sure everything was clear.

We continued on, looking at each door to see if it was the supply room. As we came close to the next corner, the lights went out – Marc got out his flashlight. At the end of the hall, a pentagram appeared on the wall in flames – sounds of voices and spirits echoed throughout. The pentagram disappeared and the lights went back on. Marc looked at me and I looked at him to make sure nothing happened to us while in the dark.

"What the hell was that?" asked Marc.

"Demons," I replied.

Both of us proceeded to the end of the hall. I started to hear something around the corner – I moved closer and got my shotgun ready. Peeking around, I saw two little demons feasting on a dead body. I came back around and prepared to engage. The demons appeared to be short. They, too, had glowing eyes and black spikes on them. I signaled Marc, silently indicating the presence of two hostiles. He acknowledged and then pointed back at me. I could tell by the look on his face something was next to me.

I slowly turned my head to the right. In the corner of my eye, I could tell something was there. I turned and faced the little beast. It snarled and tried to grab me. After I backed off, the other demon joined in.

"What the hell are those?" asked Marc.

"Those are demons, Marc," I replied.

They started to charge at us. We fired our weapons at them and they began to dissolve. Smoke rose from the eviscerated corpses and sunk into the floor. Next, another kind of demon came flying around the corner. It was a spherical creature the size of those workout gym balls. This beast had a big mouth, one red eye, two small arms, and had brain-like ridges over its body.

"What the hell is that?" asked Marc.

"Whatever it is, it doesn't seem happy."

It belched out a fireball and came straight for us. We dove out of the way in time. Marc returned fire and popped it like a balloon.

"That was easier than I expected," said Marc.

"Popped him just like a balloon," I said.

"Yeah, one with sharp teeth and wanting to kill us."

"Damn right."

After that scenario, Chris radioed us.

"Alan, Marc – Bill and I found the supply room."

"We'll be right there," I said.

We made our way to Chris and Bill. They stood next to the supply room. Chris carefully opened the door and looked inside. To my surprise, and everyone else's, the room was fairly clear. Supply lockers stood against the wall parallel to the door. It appeared safe to enter.

"Okay, Chris and I will head in while you two keep guard. We have demons running amok. Make sure none interfere," I ordered.

Chris and I entered the room. We noticed a dead guy sitting in a chair at one end but he looked like he wasn't moving anyway. I did have an uneasy feeling we may encounter zombies but who knows. Walking over to the supply lockers, we opened them up and found the EMT medical bags as well as some weapons and ammo. While we gathered the equipment, I turned to the dead guy sitting in the chair and I noticed something disturbing. The guy had no head and, I can safely say, he had it a moment ago. I tapped Chris and got his attention.

"Chris, that guy had a head before, right?" I asked.

"Yes, he did. Where did his head go?"

We went over to the corpse and inspected it. After a moment, we started hearing little tapping sounds. Out from under the supply table, we saw the head – this time with spider legs. It had blank white eyes and sharp teeth protruding from the mouth. The nose and ears seemed to be missing. Seeing this monstrosity walking around frightened us. The head began crawling and then lunged towards Chris. I wound up catching it in my hands before it got to him. Thinking fast, I threw the head to the opposite side of the room and Chris fired at it with the P-90. The head exploded into little pieces.

"What the hell was that?" asked Marc.

"You're asking me?" answered Chris.

"Some spider head thing, I guess," I replied.

"That was pretty freaky," said Bill.

"Yeah, no kidding. Now let's load up the rest of the supplies and get out of this side of Hell," I said.

We all got the remaining supplies and left. Before we could leave, the lights went out and a large flame appeared in front of the exit doors. Out from the flame came this large demon. The lights went back on. The demon stood about seven feet tall with muscle covering it from head to toe. It had two big black horns, black spikes down its arms, glowing green eyes, dark-red skin, and goat-like legs.

We hid behind the main reception counter and prepared to take on this beast. The demon gave a loud roar and raised his arms, spawning a large flame. He clapped his arms together throwing a large fireball straight at the counter. The fireball obliterated the desk and blew us back. He now had us in his sight.

"I have you now, mortals. You cannot escape," said the demon.

"What do we do?" asked Marc.

"Split up," I ordered.

We all divided and we fired from different angles. The demon threw fireballs at each of us. Thankfully, we dodged his attacks. Lesser demons started to join the party and began to overwhelm us. I ordered my buddies to take down the lesser demons while I tend to big, bad, and evil. I got up and charged towards the beast. A few of the smaller demons got in my way. They made attempts to attack but I managed to dispatch them easily. Standing before the big demon, I stared him down. He laughed and prepared to attack.

"You cannot defeat me, mortal – You are weak," said the demon.

"We'll see about that, hell-spawn."

He started to throw smaller fireballs at me in rapid succession. I dashed left and right, avoiding his projectiles. Closing in on him, I found the opportunity to strike back.

"Take this, demon scum," I shouted.

I fired my shotgun at him five times in the chest, each blast knocking him back. The demon, weakened by my attacks, began slowly dissolving. I walked up to him, grabbed him by the horns, and kneed him in the face with all my might. He fell to the floor and completely dissolved.

"Go back to Hell," I exclaimed.

My buddies finished mopping up the other enemies. Bill blasted the last demon with the six-shooter.

"Make my day, demon scum," said Bill.

"Guess I should start playing those early nineties video games a lot more," said Marc.

"Do we have everything?" I asked.

"Yep – Let's get the hell out of here," said Chris.

Chris took the bag full of supplies and we exited the station. It felt good to slay pure evil and it felt even better doing it with my friends. We put the supplies in the backseat. Marc started the van and drove off to our neighborhood to search for our friends, Mike and Charles.

MONSTER MAYHEM
7

Marc drove down Wilson Avenue and went towards Hempstead Turnpike. He went down to Gold Lane and took it to the next street. Turning right on Manor Lane, we noticed a large group of creatures further down. I told Marc to find an alternate route bypassing the area. We came to Wrench Lane and took a right. Marc stopped the van. A couple hundred feet in front of us stood a horde of creatures.

One by one, they started to notice us and began grouping together. I saw lizard men, werewolves, Minotaurs, gargoyles, demons, aliens, swamp creature-type beings, snake men, and even some female variations of those beings. We had to get out of there pronto.

"Marc, back up the van," I ordered.

"Got it," he replied.

He put the van in reverse, swung around facing the opposite direction, and floored it. I looked back and saw the creatures chasing after us, gaining fast. Marc turned right at the next street. As we drove by a tree filled area, two lizard men dropped down and started to damage the van. One of them smashed the windshield. Bill grabbed the six-shooter and fired accurate shots at them. The lizard men fell off.

"Sure Bill, F-up the van some more," said Chris.

"My mom is going to ground me for life if she sees the van like this," said Marc.

Marc made a quick right down the next street. A bulkier lizard man jumped and latched onto the right side of the van.

"We got company," exclaimed Chris.

The lizard man climbed to the top and ripped off a portion of the roof. Evan grabbed the M249 and fired at him.

"Eat this," exclaimed Evan.

He fired at him and the lizard man fell off the roof.

"Take that, scaly."

"Great, that lizard freak just put in a friggin' moonroof. How am I going to explain that?" said Marc.

"Marc, just focus on driving," ordered Laura.

"Guys, we got a big one coming," said Bill.

A gargoyle attacked us from the right side and ripped off the sliding door. As he exposed himself in the opening, I introduced him to my shotgun – the blast blew him away.

We came to the end of the street and turned right. The sound of something screeching echoed. Looking up through the hole in the roof, I saw our next enemy. This creature looked like a lizard man with wings – perhaps a dragon man?

"We got a lizard guy with wings – Marc, try and lose him," I ordered.

"She can't go any faster, captain," he replied with a Scottish accent.

The dragon guy landed on the roof and moved his way to the exposed right side of the van. He attempted to grab me but I fired back, nipping his arm. He began to attack. Evan went to assist me but got elbowed in the face. I took the base of the shotgun and swung at the creature. During my attempt, the dragon guy scratched me across my abdomen, shredding my shirt.

I tried kicking him out but, unfortunately, it didn't work. In fact, it made the situation worse. He grabbed my leg and tripped me, nearly pulling me out of the van. While trying to move away from him, I realized he put me in a vulnerable position. He went and slashed my left leg with his sharp claws – the pain was unbearable. Rebekah came around with the knife and stabbed the dragon guy in the back. Distracted by the attack, I blasted him out of the van with the shotgun.

"Argh – Medic," I said, in agonizing pain.

"Alan, status man?" asked Marc, nervously.

"I'm hit – Get us back to my house," I ordered.

"I'm on it," replied Marc.

"Get the emergency medical kit – He's bleeding badly," ordered Chris.

Laura came over to me with the EMT kit. She pulled out bandages, tape, and bottled water. Evan took some paper towels and put pressure on my leg to ease the bleeding. Laura poured water over the wound to clean it up a bit. Next, she wrapped a lot of bandages around my leg, securing it afterward with the tape.

As we made our way in the direction of my house, a Minotaur ran out from some bushes and rammed the van from the passenger side, causing us to spin out and go into a tree on someone's property. During the spin out, Laura was ejected from the van, landing on the ground behind us – she looked hurt. The van took heavy damage causing the engine to shut off. The Minotaur snarled and prepared to ram again. Not too far in the distance, some of the creatures caught up to us, a couple eyeing Laura on the ground. I had to get to her and bring her back without being a small snack for the legion. The pain in my leg concerned me but Laura needed help.

"Laura," Marc called out.

Evan jumped out of the van to take down the Minotaur while I gave out orders.

"Marc, get the van up and running – Chris, Bill, Rebekah, and Jason, defend the van – Evan, cover me," I ordered.

I grabbed the double barrel shotgun, took extra shells, and ran over to Laura. Helping her up, she, fortunately, only suffered minor injuries and could run back with no issue.

"Laura, run to the van – I've got your back," I ordered.

Laura ran back successfully and held her position. I prepared to face the onslaught of creatures. Thankfully, Evan covered me. A demon came at me and I blasted him away with the double barrel. Next, a gargoyle and werewolf came at me – I pulled the trigger and blasted both at one time. A lizard man came from the side, Evan shooting him down before he got to me. I backed off as much as I could so I wouldn't be torn to shreds.

A Minotaur came aggressively from the left and tried to smash me with his war hammer. I dove out of the way and fired at him. It didn't stop the beast but Evan got the final shots off him. After a moment of combat, Evan called out to me.

"Alan, fall back – Van is ready."

"I'm on it," I replied.

Evan came out with the minigun and gave me heavy cover fire. As I retreated, a lizard man tackled me from the side.

"I'll tear you apart human – Rrraaa," growled the lizard man.

"Get off," I exclaimed.

I held back the jaws of the lizard man while he had me pinned to the ground – his teeth sharp enough to tear flesh from the bone. Thankfully, Laura shot him off with a Beretta.

"Got your back, Alan," shouted Laura.

"Thank you – Nice shootin'," I replied.

Evan and I retreated to the van and got in.

"Get those humans," said a creature in the crowd.

"Let's get the hell out of here, man," ordered Evan.

"On our way," said Marc.

"Marc, head straight to my house – We'll lose them in the streets," I ordered.

"Roger that."

Marc got the van into gear and drove off quickly. The creatures caught up and started to attack. One creature smashed through the rear window and grabbed Jason. Laura, reacting quickly, grabbed an MP5K and fired at the creature, releasing him.

"Thanks," said Jason.

"Guys, hold them off – We're under heavy attack," exclaimed Marc.

We all fired our weapons to keep the creatures back. Chris took down some enemies from the passenger side – Bill took down an enemy trying to grab him through one of the windows – Rebekah and Laura held off enemies from the left side of the van – Lastly, I pumped buck-shot through some demons via the exposed right side.

While taking on these guys, a Minotaur came and started beating up the van from the rear. Rebekah and Laura fired at him until he stopped. After three minutes of defense, we broke free from the horde.

"We made it," said Marc.

"Thank God," said Chris.

Our foes lie dead behind us. Now we could retreat to my house to hold a position. A few of us needed medical attention. Within a few minutes, we made it. Marc drove up my driveway and we all got out.

"Alright guys, let's secure my house, and then take it easy. Bring some weapons in, too," I ordered.

"If anyone needs first aid, Laura and I will patch you up," said Marc.

We all went inside and walked into the living room, settling down on the couches.

"Where the hell did these freaks come from?" asked Rebekah.

"I don't know, but at least we have a break now," said Laura.

"Does anyone else need first aid?" asked Marc.

After Marc finished patching up the others, we took it easy. It started to get dark out and we all needed to rest. Before I went to sleep, Marc mentioned to me he and a few others would take shifts staying up to keep watch. I made myself comfortable on the couch and slowly dozed off.

In the middle of the night, I woke up to hear a tapping sound. Looking around my family room, I only saw my friends sleeping. Someone should've been awake to keep watch. I heard the tapping again and looked to see a shadowy figure up through the skylight. The figure scurried away and I heard it moving on the roof. I got my shotgun and prepared to investigate. As I walked to the family room door, I accidentally woke Chris up.

"Alan?"

"Chris, something is walking around on the roof."

"Are you serious?"

"I saw something through the skylight and I'm hearing movement."

We started hearing some movement on the roof. Chris felt uneasy about the situation.

"Dammit – This isn't good – Do you want me to go with you?" he asked.

"No, stay here. I want you to guard everyone. If I'm not back in ten minutes, wake Marc and Evan. Hopefully, I won't run into major trouble. Plus, I'll try not to blow our cover."

"Be careful – I don't want to see you dismembered if I go and find you."

"I'll be as careful as I can be."

I followed the sound of movement towards the front of the house, leading into the kitchen. A calm wind blew in from my broken windows – the blinds swaying in the breeze. I carefully proceeded into my kitchen staying as quiet as I can. Suddenly, a shadow cast on the wall opposite me. The shadow moved away and disappeared. Carefully moving over to the window, I took a quick glance. There appeared to be nothing but the still, dark night. The moon loomed in the sky, its rays casting little light. I made my way over to the side door and opened it. If something had discovered our position, it was going to be a long night.

I exited my house and closed the door behind me. My eyes darted left and right, looking for movement. I carefully moved my way further out. My nerves high – fear pulsing through my veins. I felt something was watching me – watching every move I made and waiting for the right moment to attack. I turned rapidly in all directions making sure the area was clear. After a moment, I heard a voice.

"We know what you seek."

The voice sounded female. I didn't know if someone or something was there. My mind could've been playing tricks on me.

"Who's there?"

"We don't mean harm."

"We?"

"Put down your weapon. We only want to speak to you."

"Okay – If I put down my gun, will you not surprise or attack me?"

No one answered – I felt really nervous. It's dark, quiet, and spooky. All I heard was my heart beating hard and fast. In a blink of an eye, something threw a chain out from the shadows, wrapping around my gun, and yanking it out of my hands. Afterwards, something grabbed me from behind and covered my mouth. I struggled a bit until the individual spoke.

"Shh, calm down. I'm not going to hurt you, human. All we ask is that you listen to us."

Agreeing to her request, she let me go. The being walked in front of me – it was a female gargoyle with pale blue skin and white hair. Her eyes glowed brightly and looked straight at me.

Soon after, other creatures started emerging from the shadows. I saw a lizard man, a lizard woman, a Minotaur, a female Minotaur, a male gargoyle, and a snake woman. I wondered what they needed to tell me.

"We need to speak to you. I apologize for the scare but we were unsure about your reaction to us," said the female gargoyle.

"That's fine – As long as you don't hurt me, I'm okay with it."

"We've come to warn you that the Master's minions are coming – You must leave tomorrow," she started saying, "He has been informed that you weren't captured. An assault squad will be coming around noon tomorrow to get you and your friends."

"Even worse, they may slaughter you," added the lizard man.

"Question – Why are all of you helping me?" I asked.

"We are against our Master. He uses fear to force individuals, like ourselves, to slaughter people even though we have no intention to do so," explained the lizard man.

"Once we heard about a group of humans running loose, we thought we can speak to you and ask for your assistance to help end this war," said the female gargoyle.

"After seeing what happened earlier today, we knew we have found an excellent group of heroes," added the female Minotaur.

"You all saw what happened?"

"Indeed we did," said the male gargoyle.

"How is the wound on your leg?" the female gargoyle asked.

"It still hurts – The dragon guy got me pretty bad."

"Let me see the wound – I have special medicine for it," said the lizard man.

He walked over to me and I removed a bit of the bandage. Taking out this pouch full of this paste-like substance, he scooped up a bit and applied it to the wound. To my surprise, the pain went away and I felt better.

"This is a paste containing ground up Taku berries – It has healing abilities that sterilize the wound and ease the pain. It also increases the speed of healing," explained the lizard man.

"Wow – Thank you."

After the lizard man walked back over to the female gargoyle, I went and asked a question,

"If you don't mind me asking, where did all of you come from? Are you from Earth or did you come from another planet?"

"We come from Earth – We're from the island of Anthronia – It's located in the Atlantic Ocean. The only beings not from Earth are the Clymerians. They are the blue creatures you have seen. Their origin is a planet called Tenorah-Helias," the lizard woman explained.

"How come I've never heard of or even seen your island on a map?"

"Your governments avoided putting Anthronia on maps so people would never know of our existence. Our ancestors were exiled to this island over a millennium ago," said the female gargoyle.

"Humans don't want us around," said the Minotaur.

"They don't even want to look at us," added the female Minotaur.

"Many say we are hideous, but what do they know?" said the snake woman.

"Hey, you guys are fine from my standpoint," I started to say, "It's the inside that matters the most, not the outside. Unfortunately, humans look on the outside with everything. Once they look at you and see that you're different, they think of you as a freak. Even with a regular human like myself, I've been prejudged, too. People made fun of me because I was different. Believe me – I know what it's like to be outcasted."

    The group was pleased to see I understood their perspective – they weren't so different from humans. They can walk, talk, and feel emotions just like any ordinary person. Human society sees these creatures as monsters, however, humans appear to be the aggressors out of all this. Humanity exiled these creatures because they were different. Fear and anger turned humanity into monsters. This must be the reason for the invasion. It was Anthronia's way to combat years of discrimination. Being cry-bullies obviously made the situation worse.

"It is time for us to go," said the male gargoyle, looking at the position of the moon.

"Before we leave, we want to warn you of a massive creature the Master has unleashed. He calls it Destructa. Be on the lookout for this vile creation," said the Minotaur.

"Thanks for the heads-up."

The lizard man gave me my shotgun back and I thanked him. The female gargoyle came over to me.

"We wish you luck, human," she said, presenting a necklace with an eye shaped emblem.

"What's this?"

"The Guardian Emblem – May it protect you on your journey – It is the eye of justice."

She placed the necklace on me.

"May the spirits of fate guide you to victory."

"My team and I will do our best."

"We know you can do it."

"It's up to you to make peace between our two worlds. We need heroes in this corrupt world. You all are our last hope for the survival of both the human race and our species," said the male gargoyle.

"Rest up – You have a big day tomorrow. If you successfully reach Anthronia, stop our Master at all costs," said the lizard man.

"Will do."

As they began leaving, the lizard woman came over to me.

"Good luck – Maybe we'll meet again," she said.

The lizard woman brushed her tail up against me, gave me a wink, and grinned. She then walked off, following the rest of the group. It appeared she may have been interested in me. With my luck, I wouldn't be surprised if my future girlfriend would be a humanoid reptile. While waving goodbye to the group, Marc came up to me from behind along with Chris and Evan. They had been watching for the past ten minutes and were already aware of the plan for tomorrow.

We went back in and slept for the remaining part of the evening. I had an alarm clock set to go off around 5:00 AM. Tomorrow marked the next chapter in our adventure – the journey to Anthronia.

ONE WAY TICKET TO ANTHRONIA
8

The alarm went off at 5:00 AM. I woke up feeling much better – the Taku berry paste actually helped a lot. My wound had healed and the pain was very benign. I stretched my legs and walked around a bit. Afterwards, I began waking everyone up.

"Alright everyone, rise and shine – We got a big day – Let's get done," I ordered.

Everybody freshened up and had breakfast. After they had finished, we met back in the family room and began discussing the main objective for the day.

"Alright everyone, may I have your attention please?" I started to say, "Okay, we must discuss what we need to accomplish today. First off, I encountered a group of friendly creatures last night. These beings enlightened me on what is going on. First, they told me we have to be out of here before noon. Second, the source of the invasion came from this island in the Atlantic called Anthronia. So far, it helps us a bit but still, we need to know how we are going to get there. Obviously we need air transportation, however, we have no clue where Anthronia is on global coordinates."

"Alan, I thought of this idea last night with the device I have in the van," started Marc, "I was thinking of converting it into this Scan-Lock system. I should be able to convert it into that with the tools we've acquired. Once constructed, we should be able to pick up a radio frequency the creatures are using to communicate from Anthronia to here. Of course, I have to amp it up so it can receive a large-scale radius of the area. Hopefully, I can get it to scan up to one hundred miles, which should be the approximate length of Long Island."

"Excellent idea, Marc," I said.

Marc's idea seemed to be our best option. During the timeframe we had, he had to complete this within an hour or two. Knowing him, I knew he would be able to create the Scan-Lock system successfully.

Our next objective was to retrieve our two friends, Mike, the navigator, and Charles, the martial artist. After I finished the briefing, Marc got down to work. I brought him the toolbox and other supplies he needed to complete the Scan-Lock system. While he worked on the project, Chris, Bill, and I started modifying the metal pieces they found in the department store parking lot. We molded the pieces into knee pads, shoulder pads, and some shin guards. While everyone geared up, Jason and Laura joined to help Marc expedite the construction of the system. Chris then approached me about an issue regarding the occupancy of the van,

"Alan, I noticed that we may not be able to fit everyone in the van. There might not be enough room."

"Good point, Chris. Evan and Rebekah, would you be able to remove the rear seats of the van and the ones near the sliding doors?"

"Yeah, we can do that," replied Evan.

"Good. Let's get down to that now. Chris and Bill, cover Evan and Rebekah. Keep your eyes peeled for any hostiles."

"Got it," said Bill.

Evan and Rebekah proceeded to remove the detachable seats in the van – the driver and passenger seat remained. After they finished, the van can now fit everyone inside comfortably. In addition, we had the ability to store most of the weapons in compartments built into the floor. The only weapon we couldn't fit in these storage compartments was the minigun – it remained in the rear of the van. Afterwards, we went back into my house and waited for Marc to be done. Within an hour, the Scan-Lock system had been successfully constructed.

"Guys, it's done," said Marc.

"Fire that thing up and let's see what we get," said Chris.

Marc activated the system and turned a few dials.

"I may have to adjust the antenna to get different signals but, I believe it should work."

We started hearing some garbled radio frequencies. Jason came over and did some adjustments. Soon we started hearing the frequency the creatures used.

"Are the humans secure at the hangar?" said one creature.

"Yes, the AOK airport hangar is secured, sir," said another.

"The battle cruiser is on its way. It should arrive there at noon."

"When are those cruisers going to become faster, why are they always slow?"

"Well, this is what the Clymerians gave us so deal with it. I spoke with the master and he said everything is going as planned."

"I tell you, why didn't we do this invasion years ago? Getting payback on the humans is incredible."

"Anyway, sergeant, tell your men to be on their guard and make sure no human escapes."

"Roger that."

The system began to overheat and then shut off. Thankfully, it did that after we heard what we needed to hear.

"So, they are at AOK airport," said Bill.

"We got to stop that cargo from boarding that cruiser," said Evan.

"No, we can't stop it," I said.

"...and why not?"

"If we stop the boarding, we can't get to the source of the invasion. We must board that cruiser unseen so we can head to the home base of the mastermind," I said.

Many felt uneasy about the plan. We needed to hitch a ride on a cruiser to get to Anthronia. The time was 8:15 AM and we needed to be at the airport before noon. It would take approximately forty-five minutes to an hour to get to AOK airport from my house. I told everyone to get ready to depart. Our objective for the moment: Retrieve Mike and Charles.

We boarded the van and Marc started backing out of the driveway. First stop: Mike's house. As soon as we got there, Chris, Bill, and I went to go get him.

"Okay guys, it'll just be me, Bill, and Chris. We'll go in and find Mike."

We entered his house from the side door entrance into the kitchen. Plenty of broken glass and belongings littered the floor. Before proceeding further in, we heard a sound coming from under the sink. Bill carefully opened the little cabinet door and, to our surprise, it was Mike.

"Hey, Mike," said Chris.

"Chris, Bill, Alan? What happened around here?" asked Mike.

"Mike, the whole area has been invaded by strange, humanoid, creatures," I replied.

"Creatures?"

"Yes – We all are going to infiltrate the AOK airport and board this cruiser that will lead us to the mastermind of the invasion."

"Let's get to it."

We exited the house and went back to the van. Our next stop was Charles' house. Marc drove down Wrench Lane in the direction of Hempstead Turnpike. On our way, we saw Charles walking down the street – Marc stopped the vehicle.

"Hey, Charles," I called out.

"No way – You guys are alive? Yes," said Charles, with excitement.

"There's no time to waste, Charles. Today, we are going to go after the mastermind of the invasion. Hop in – We'll explain."

Charles came in and found a seat. Before we drove off, I pointed over to a wooden board on the street. I asked Charles if he can bring it over. I thought we could use it as a makeshift door for the exposed side of the van. After securing the board with tons of duct tape Marc had lying around, we then ventured off. During this time, a few of us explained to Mike and Charles the situation and what we will be doing when we arrive at the airport.

I looked around the van and saw many who were scared but ready. As Marc got onto the highway, he floored it. Unfortunately, the van couldn't go too fast because of the damages. We'll settle for seventy-five miles per hour.

Passing some urban areas, we saw more destruction. Fires raged on large structures and the air smelled polluted. The sight of a desolate skyline didn't help our spirits. While driving along, a large shadow appeared on the ground followed by the sound of a loud roar. I looked up through the roof of the van and saw something I'd never imagine seeing.

"What is that?" asked Marc.

"It's a freakin' dragon – Evan, get the minigun ready," I exclaimed.

Death from above – this had to be Destructa. Evan set up the minigun and loaded the chain of bullets in. Before he poked his head through the roof, the dragon blew a puff of fire, just missing us.

"Man, that was close," said Evan.

"Hang on tight everyone," I said.

The dragon roared and blew another puff – this time it was closer.

"Evan, shoot the damn thing," shouted Marc.

Evan prepared the gun and pointed it upward. Charles and I held him so he didn't lose his balance.

"It's time to turn this dragon into a leaky piece of meat," Evan said, pulling the trigger.

The barrels of the gun began to rotate, building up speed in a matter of seconds.

"Say your prayers, biatch."

Evan fired the minigun and hit the dragon hard. A puff of fire came at us and Marc swerved out of the way.

"Damn, that was close," said Evan.

"Keep shooting," exclaimed Marc.

Evan continued to fire at the dragon. It came down and hit the van from the left side. The van tilted and I ordered everyone to move the weight to the left. Thankfully, we stabilized the van successfully.

Evan fired the last of the rounds and defeated our flying foe. Our adventure wasn't over yet, however. A dying dragon was coming in for a crash-landing. Marc pushed the van as much as he could to escape the impact.

"Come on baby, don't let me down."

We successfully pulled away as the dragon crashed down on the roadway. There was a sigh of relief in the van. We all relaxed for the time being until we got to the airport. Twenty minutes passed and we had arrived. Exiting the van, I told my friends to line up and face me while I talk to them for a moment. I looked around at everyone and all seemed nervous, yet ready for action.

"Okay everyone, this is a one-shot deal. Main objective: Board that cruiser at all costs. It's time to prove not only each other what you're made of but to prove to these creatures that we mean business. It's time to save humanity – Are you ready?"

"Waiting for orders," said Marc.

"I'm ready," said Charles.

"Ready for action," said Evan.

"Let's rock," said Bill.

"Let's get 'em," said Mike.

"Ready, sir," said Laura.

"Ready," said Rebekah.

"Ready," said Chris.

"Ready," said Jason.

"Okay, the time is ten-thirty AM. Let's move in," I said, pointing towards the entrance.

We all approached the building entrance and entered quietly. I told everyone to stay low and to locate a nearby security office if they see one. While inside, we found many people dead – some were fallen SWAT team members. Bill tapped my shoulder...

"Alan, I see the security office over there."

I gave a hand signal to everyone to follow. Entering the office, we found a security guard on the floor dead. He seemed to have suffered a critical injury around his neck. We proceeded in carefully and the coast appeared to be clear.

"Marc, see if you can get into the security system. Look through some of the cameras and let me know what you find. Chris, Bill, and Mike – Search through the office to see if there are any useful items or equipment. Evan and Charles, secure the perimeter of this office. Jason, Rebekah, and Laura – Obtain weapons and gear from the SWAT team members," I ordered.

All acknowledged and proceeded with their designated objectives. I joined in with Chris, Bill, and Mike to help them locate useful items. While looking around, Marc came over and informed me he had found something on one of the monitors.

"We have some hostiles guarding a particular area. The cam indicates it's viewing gate twenty. They're probably guarding the area where the cruiser may be landing."

"Though it seems – Okay, let's proceed down to that area. If we can sneak past those guards, we may be able to get out onto the tarmac."

"How are we going to do that undetected?"

"That is the million-dollar question. We have several armed hostiles who may call for backup or inform their master about us."

"Do you think a diversion is possible?"

"That may be the only option. Let's get Chris, Bill, and Mike over here – Let's see what they say."

I went over and got the three. Marc gave them the low down of our current predicament. I asked them what strategy would be appropriate for this scenario.

"We can probably use an emergency exit to gain access outside. Is there a fire emergency floor plan map available?" asked Chris.

"Got it right here," Mike replied.

Mike analyzed the floor plan and then spoke.

"Okay, we are here. This is where the nearest exits are. The only problem is that these exits will lead us on the wrong side of the tarmac. If I'm not mistaken, there are fences that separate civilian access and personnel access."

"If it helps, there are still a lot of things that can give us cover from the guards. If you look on screen, there's luggage everywhere, garbage pales thrown around, and even some areas where we could hide," said Marc.

"It's a risky idea but we'll have to play this like chess. The guards aren't in one spot for long. They appear to stand in one position and then move to another spot," I said.

"If we time their movements just right, we could get past them."

"I've been watching them on the monitor and see that they change their spot every thirty seconds," said Bill.

"Has it been consistent?" I asked.

"So far, it has for the past couple minutes," he replied.

"Alright, let's get ready to head there."

We exited the office to regroup with the rest. Chris, Marc, and I informed everyone about the situation. All of them understood what we had to do. Jason, Rebekah, and Laura obtained the armored vests from the SWAT team as well as extra weapons, ammo, and walkie-talkies. We equipped ourselves with the armored vests and got our weapons ready. Before proceeding to gate twenty, we heard something coming from behind a trash can and some luggage. I went to go check it out and, to my surprise, there were two humanoid dogs.

"Hey, what's the big idea?" one asked.

"You can talk?" I questioned.

"Yeah, I can talk, so can my brother here."

For a moment, my friends and I were both fascinated and freaked out that a bipedal, two foot tall, dog was actually talking to us.

"So, who are you guys and what are you doing here?" the dog asked.

"My name is Alan and these are my friends. We are on a journey to locate the mastermind of the invasion," I replied.

"Are you really? I wouldn't mind teaching that mastermind a thing or two for causing all this mayhem," he said.

"Yeah, dude," added the other dog.

While introducing everyone else, I could tell these two were quite intrigued.

"Nice to meet you all. Looks like your friends are still looking at us in disbelief that a couple of dogs, like us, can talk. Anyway, my name is Lucky and this here is my brother Rollus – Everyone calls him Roller."

"Hey, dudes," said Roller.

"So, you're looking for the gate where it leads to the airfield or something? I overheard some of those guards they got humans locked up in one of them hangars," said Lucky.

"We saw in the security office there were guards covering an area around gate twenty. Would you be able to guide us there?" I asked.

"Sure, we'll get you guys down there. Can we tag along with you on your journey? After what these monstrosities did to these innocent people, we wouldn't mind teaching these freaks a lesson."

"Of course you can. I'm curious, do you have any special skills?"

"Hell yeah, man. I'm able to hack through security systems and doors. I am also able to hack into secured computers. How I'm able to do all this, you ask, is through this little hacking device."

Lucky pulled out this small electronic device, similar to a PDA – it looked quite sophisticated. Lucky seemed like he knew a lot about security systems – certainly, his skill would come in handy when we need it.

"I'm quite impressed, Lucky. What does your brother do?" I asked.

"I know a lot about meteorology and aviation. I also like being out in nature chilling with herbal tea, dude," replied Roller.

"Yeah and I believe you had too much of that herbal tea," said Lucky.

"Dude, it was green tea with special herbs in it."

"Man, I believe it was weed in there, homes."

A couple of us chuckled at this little comical scenario. It seemed Lucky and Roller were quite cartoon-like. Lucky's voice closely resembled a favorite comedian of mine – one who spoke fast and had a high voice. His brother, Roller, had more of a surfer-like voice – always saying "dude" before or after every sentence. After they finished their little sibling rivalry, I gave both a Glock pistol.

"Once I come across the scumbag who sent these fools here, I'll go gangsta on his ass," said Lucky.

"In time, Luck. I do have one question for you, though. Did you guys come from Anthronia?"

"Anthronia? No way, man. My bro and I actually were experiments of this mad scientist guy. Long story short, we started out as Labrador Retrievers and then Doc morphed us into bipedal subjects. Our brains, too, were modified to be more like a human's. So, yeah – We're friggin' freaks of nature."

"How did you two get here? Shouldn't you be in a lab?" asked Marc.

"Funny story, man – We were confiscated by security a few years ago when Frankenstein tried to bring us on a plane. Fortunately, one of the security guards adopted us. From that point on, we learned many things about technology, security systems, and so on."

"Quite interesting, Lucky," I said.

"Stories aside, let's get down to gate twenty," said Lucky.

We proceeded towards our destination, keeping a watchful eye out for any hostiles. Closing in on the gate entrance, a few guards patrolled the area. We hid behind some seats and luggage, hoping the guards don't see us. After they changed their position, we quietly snuck around a guard distracted by an electronic device he had. We made our way down the gate tunnel. At the end, there was no ladder or stairway to get down – only a twenty-foot drop to the landing field.

"Great, how are we going to get down?" asked Jason.

"I think we may need to find an alternate route," said Marc.

"Do you think we can jump down?" I asked.

"Alan that is a twenty-foot drop – You are going to hurt yourself – We need another idea."

"Maybe if we had a rope we…" Chris started to say.

Bill revealed a rope after Chris suggested the idea. Everyone was bewildered on where he got a long line of rope.

"Where did you find this, Bill?" asked Chris.

"I don't know, just found it. Perhaps the author put it here…"

Bill gave me the rope and I tied it to an area in the tunnel. Thankfully, it was long enough.

We climbed down and hid behind a luggage carrier. Peeking around, I noticed guards holding a position near a hangar with the number eighteen on it. We took a path around some cargo boxes and other airfield vehicles. Making our way to the main hangar, we went towards the back door and got ready to enter.

"Evan and Charles, proceed in first," I ordered.

"Got it," replied Evan.

"Roger," replied Charles.

The two opened the door carefully and proceeded in. Evan and Charles gave the okay. As we entered, we hid behind some crates and barrels. Beyond the crates, I saw a few small towers of cages with people in them – tarps covered the lower portion of them as they stood atop special transport carts. I looked all around making sure there were no guards present. After I checked, I got everyone together and explained what we're going to do.

"Okay guys, there doesn't seem to be any guards securing the inside of this hangar. Also, I found our one-way ticket onto that cruiser," I said.

"Seeing there are transport carts standing by, I'm guessing we hitch a ride on one of those so we can sneak in undetected," said Chris.

"Exactly – Now let's find a spot on them. We can cover ourselves with the tarps. I can hear the cruiser coming closer and I believe it is a bit earlier than noon. Proceed to the carts now. Stay low and stay quiet until further orders. Chris and Laura – Take a walkie-talkie and standby with a few," I ordered.

We all got in the first row of carts. The ones we occupied were connected to each other. This means all of us would get in the cruiser at the same time. I was in the front car with Marc, Charles, Evan, and Lucky. The sound of the cruiser getting closer was quite audible. I took a peek out through the tarp and the hangar door began to open. After it opened all the way, I could see the cruiser coming in for a landing.

This ship was half the size of a football field. None of us have ever seen anything this big. Like a Chinook helicopter, it opened its hatch door from beneath it. From the opening came a utility vehicle. It appeared to be the one to tow the carts into the ship. The vehicle approached the hangar and proceeded to our set first. A couple of creatures came out and hooked the carts up to it. After locking everything in place, the vehicle started pulling us out. Getting close to this gargantuan cruiser, my heart started beating harder and faster.

After entering the cruiser, it took about twenty minutes for the vehicle to finish towing in all the carts. The hatch door began closing and we could hear the engines starting up. My friends and I felt extremely scared. I took a deep breath and tried to remain focused. This was it – Anthronia could possibly be our final destination.

When we arrive there, who knows if we will succeed or face our unfortunate doom. So many things were going through my mind – I felt overwhelmed. We remained quiet and tried to keep calm. The hatch door closed all the way and the engines were at full power – the ship then took off. We had a long flight ahead of us. Now, we wait…

ANTHRONIA
9

It took an hour for the cruiser to arrive on Anthronia. The ship began to tremble during our descent to the island. I tried to remain calm and not get too nervous – who wasn't nervous? We all prepared ourselves for anything to come. After a successful landing, the hatch door opened. A few towing vehicles came up the platform and assisted pulling out the cargo. One of the towing vehicles came to move our cart out. Taking a peek from under the tarp, I saw a magnificent island with a lot of vegetation – palm trees, exotic plants, flowers and other beautiful features. Evan decided to take a peek at his end and saw something interesting.

"Guys, this place looks like a city within a rainforest. Really, it's about half the size of Manhattan."

We came over to look. A large city can be seen from beyond the vegetation. The buildings towered over the trees – certainly a sight to behold.

"My God, you're right," said Marc.

Within twenty minutes, we made it into the city. The streets were populated by a variety of anthropomorphic beings. Who knew they lived similarly to our lifestyle. There were stores, businesses, and apartment buildings.

"Looks like loincloths are the style here," said Marc.

"Must feel kind of funny walking around almost naked," said Charles.

"To us, it may seem odd – To them, it's an everyday thing," I said.

"The ladies look pretty nice – Yeah, love that booty, girl," said Lucky.

About ten minutes had passed going through the city. The carts came to a halt. Something did not seem right. I decided to radio Laura since she was closer to the towing vehicle.

"Laura, what's the status at your end?"

"By the looks of it, they're examining the cargo. The first set of carts doesn't have anyone in it but they're looking under the tarps," she replied.

"Crap – You, Jason, and Rebekah carefully and quietly get out of there and hide near an alleyway," I ordered.

"Roger that," she replied.

I radioed Chris and gave him a heads up. Since the part of the city we occupied wasn't congested, we didn't have to worry about any bystanders stopping us.

"Alright, let's quietly escape," I said.

As Marc, Evan, Charles, Lucky and I climbed out of the cart, further down, Jason tripped over Rebekah and Laura, blowing our cover.

"Alert – Humans escaping," shouted one guard.

"Get them," shouted another.

A few guards started coming after us. My friends up front got captured. We ran in the opposite direction but a couple of guards caught up. Both grabbed Evan and Charles.

"Get off me," shouted Charles.

"Quiet down monkey – You're coming with us," the guard exclaimed.

"Let me go, man," exclaimed Evan.

"Shut up," said the other guard.

Marc, Lucky, and I ran until we heard a pop sound. Within a matter of seconds, an explosion occurred from behind, knocking us down hard. My ears rang – I felt disoriented and weak. Before I blacked out, I saw big tan-colored feet in front of me and heard this individual speak with a deep voice,

"Are you alright? Hang on – I'll get you some help."

I fell unconscious. Whoever was there to assist, I hoped they were taking us somewhere safe.

I don't know how long I was out. When I regained consciousness, I noticed my vision was blurry. I felt confused and scared. My breathing was a little fast but I calmed down after I felt someone gently petting my head. I then heard a sweet and gentle voice of a woman next to the bed I was on.

"Are you alright, sweetie?" she asked.

I turned to the woman – I sensed she was quite concerned about my well-being.

"Here, drink some water," she said.

She lifted my head and I took a few sips. The cool water against my lips felt good. My eyes started clearing up and my vision became better. I could now see the woman. She had green, reptilian skin with a yellowish midsection, wore a magenta-colored outfit reminiscent of an Indian sari, had amber colored eyes with slit pupils, and seemed quite young, probably around my age – maybe between sixteen and eighteen.

"Where am I?" I asked.

"You're in my friend's apartment. He brought you here after you were injured badly," she replied,

"Here, drink some more water."

I drank some more and started to regain my strength.

"Thank you."

"Are you feeling better? You were out for a few hours."

"I was out that long?"

She nodded yes.

"Man, I must have taken one hell of a beating."

"When my friend brought you in, we thought we had lost you. Thank goodness you're alive. Are you doing okay?" she asked, placing her hand my shoulder.

"I believe so — The water helped a lot."

"By the way, my name's Sandra."

"Pleasure to meet you, Sandra — My name is Alan."

We shook hands — she seemed very nice.

"I'm surprised you aren't in shock of my appearance. I hear humans usually get freaked out."

"You look fine, Sandra. I don't see you as scary or monstrous. All I see is a very kind and caring person."

Sandra giggled a little — I could tell she appreciated my well-mannered behavior.

"Is there anything I can get you, Alan?" she asked.

"No, thank you — I do have one question though…"

I noticed under the covers, I had no clothes on. Yep, butt naked under a blanket in front of a girl — awkward…

"I'm curious — Do you know where my clothes are?" I asked, bashfully.

"They're right over on the dresser. They're a little ripped and burnt — That's how my friend found you," she replied.

"I see."

"Anyway, my friend Talmar will check in on you shortly. He's the one who bandaged you up."

Suddenly, the door to the room opened. In the doorway stood a tan-colored gargoyle — he appeared to be about six and a half feet tall. He walked over next to Sandra and looked down at me. His eyes glowed like headlights on a car.

"Finally, he's up," he said.

"Brooke, this is Alan. Alan, this is Brooke," said Sandra.

"Nice to meet you, kid."

I shook Brooke's hand. Compared to Sandra's handshake, Brooke had one hell of a grip. I thought I was going to have another injury.

"It's pleasure to meet you, Brooke."

"I'm surprised you're not freaking out."

"Believe me, I feel quite comfortable around you guys – Seeing that you're friendly and all."

"You're the first human I've ever seen not afraid. All the others run in fear from me despite I've saved them."

"Well, the ones that ran away are normal humans. I'm your, quote-unquote, not so normal human."

My little joke made Sandra and Brooke chuckle a little – I could tell they liked me.

"Listen, guys, I'm going to head inside to check up on the others," said Brooke.

"Others? Who else did you pick up?" I asked.

"There was one other human and this dog guy – Both of them suffered concussions."

"Are both okay?"

"Yeah, they are still knocked out but, overall, they're fine."

"Excellent – Good to know that – Thank you."

"I'll be back guys."

Brooke left the room and closed the door.

"So, yeah, your friends inside are doing fine," said Sandra.

Before Sandra and I resumed our conversation, her other friend came in. This individual was a lizard man in doctor's apparel, wore glasses resting atop of his snout, had blue skin, green eyes, and stood about six feet tall.

"Hello, I see the human has awakened," he said with a British accent.

"Talmar, this is Alan. Alan, this is Talmar."

"It's pleasure to meet you, Alan."

"It's pleasure to meet you, too, Talmar."

After shaking his hand, I was pleased with his well-mannered demeanor. Compared to others of his species, he seemed well-educated and civilized.

"Alan, Talmar is going to do a brief checkup. It shouldn't take too long, right Talmar?"

"Not at all. I'll be taking a look at his injuries and making sure everything is healing correctly. If need be, I will distribute antibiotics for some of the wounds."

"Sounds good – I'll be back."

Sandra left the room and closed the door.

"Alright, Alan, I'll just need you to sit up."

Talmar did some basic tests like listening to my heart and breathing. While he performed tests on me, I could overhear Sandra and Brooke talking in the other room. I couldn't hear them well so there will probably be a temporary perspective change – queue third person mode! Whoosh!

* * * * * * *

While Talmar examined Alan, Sandra and Brooke talked to each other in the living room.

"So, Al's alright?" asked Brooke.

"Yep – Talmar is currently examining him," replied Sandra.

"It's interesting that Alan is the only human I came across who is not one bit nervous around us. Also, it's surprising he didn't ask if we were going to eat him. Back in New York, when I rescued people, they always asked 'Are you going to eat me?' Heh, it's nice to not hear that for once."

"I'm surprised how nice he is – He's so polite and respectful – In a way, I think he's kind of cute, too."

Brooke puts his arm around Sandra.

"Sandra, what are you?"

"A Najanian…"

"…and what is he?"

"A human…"

"Good, I'm glad you clarified the main difference between you two."

"Brooke, he may be just a human but I've dated other guys who aren't my kind, too."

"True, but I don't feel a human would be into you. Does he feel the same way about you? You were speaking to the guy for at least five minutes."

"I don't know, Brooke. I felt something within him – some kind of energy – a positive aura of some sort."

"Spend more time with him – Maybe you'll find out what that energy is. In the meantime, let's go grab something to drink – It may be a long night."

Sandra and Brooke went to the kitchen to get something to drink and sat down at the table. Back in the bedroom, Talmar finished examining Alan. Queue first-person mode! Whoosh!

* * * * * * *

Talmar had just finished examining my physical status and proceeded to look at my wounds. He put some Taku berry paste on the part of me that got burned from the explosion. He then began examining the wound on my left leg.

"If you don't mind me asking, Alan, what happened to your leg?"

"My friends and I were escaping a legion of opposition and I was attacked by a dragon-guy. He slashed my leg badly."

"Oh my, that must have been quite painful."

"Oh, yeah – It hurt like hell."

"By the way, the dragon-like being is called a Draiycon. They are usually seen in the Anthronian military as higher-ups."

"So, that's what they're called."

"Indeed – What really frightens me about this invasion is that the Clymerians were involved."

"A friendly group of Anthronian denizens informed me about the Clymerians. Do you know more about them? I, too, heard word of them on a radio transmission."

"The president of this island created an alliance with these beings. They're a very advanced extraterrestrial race – Highly violent and tyrannical – The queen most of all."

"No kidding."

"Tis the dark age, sadly. It is a horrible feeling to be afraid. This world doesn't provide much security anymore, especially with the one who masterminded the invasion of your territory. What we need are heroes to bring light into this world."

"Indeed – Right now, I'm worried about my friends. I have no idea where they were taken – I hope they're okay."

"No need to worry, Alan. I feel confident they're alright. Tomorrow, we'll try and figure out a way to find your friends and perhaps locate the fiend responsible for this chaos."

"Thank you, Talmar – I appreciate your assistance."

"You're very welcome, Alan – Rest well, my friend."

    Talmar finished re-wrapping my leg. He left the room and I relaxed. I heard him inform Sandra and Brooke everything went well with the examination. Within a minute, Sandra entered.

"Hey – I heard everything is okay."

"Yes, thankfully – I couldn't believe it myself – After what I went through, I thought I would have broken bones or internal injuries."

"I'm glad you're okay. Did you want anything to eat or drink?"

"Maybe a little water – I am quite thirsty."

Sandra retrieved the glass of water sitting on the dresser.

"Here you go."

"Thank you."

After taking a few sips, I placed the cup on the nightstand next to the bed. I noticed Sandra taking a few glances at me.

"May I ask you a question, Alan?"

"Sure."

"Back in your home territory, did you have a girlfriend?" she asked bashfully.

"No, unfortunately – Believe me, human girls are very picky. They want the cool guys, not the nerds."

"Aww…I don't think you're a nerd."

"Well, I am – A different kind, though."

Sandra chuckled,

"So, you only have regular friends?"

"Yes – We all journeyed here to figure out what invaded our town. Most of them were captured and I don't know where they were taken. If I ever get a chance to introduce you to my friends, I'm sure you'll like them and I'm sure they'll like you and your friends."

"Really?"

"I'm quite sure they wouldn't have a problem with you – I don't think there would be any issue because you're a very sweet person, Sandra. If I like you, my friends should, too."

Sandra seemed flattered – she smiled and gazed at me.

"You're a very sweet guy, Alan. It's strange why human females have no interest in you."

"As mentioned, they want the 'cool' guys – You know, the ones who are fit and attract the ladies from afar with their good looks."

"I think you're fine the way you are."

"You really think so?"

"Yeah – It's what's on the inside that matters the most, not the outside. I think others should not judge by look but judge by understanding who they are. If people were to see it that way, there would be so much peace and love in the world."

"You are absolutely right, Sandra. Maybe both humans and the other species on this island would get along and there would be no war between the two sides. In addition, my friends and I wouldn't have to walk through Hell."

"Aww – I could imagine how horrifying it was for all of you. No one should endure that. Tomorrow, Talmar, Brooke, and I will help you find your friends."

"Thank you."

"You're very brave, Alan."

Sandra placed her right hand over my chest – she felt my heartbeat.

"You have a strong heart – I can feel courage and generosity within you," she said while analyzing my heart rhythms.

"How can you tell?" I asked.

"It's nice, strong, and has a normal pace. A heart like this is something special – this is a heart of gold."

She felt my heart for a minute longer and then gently placed her hand on my right hand. Our eyes met – we smiled at each other, living in the moment. Both of us started to feel a connection with one another. I know some people would say, "Alan, she's an ugly lizard girl." At this moment, I didn't care what Sandra looked like. While looking deep into her amber eyes, I could see the most beautiful girl in front of me. Brooke then knocked on the door and entered.

"Okay, guys, time to head to sleep," said Brooke.

"Okay – Are you comfortable, Alan?" asked Sandra.

"Yes, quite comfortable, thank you," I replied.

"Get a good rest," she said while placing her hand on my shoulder.

"Sandra..."

"Yes?"

"I want to thank you for your hospitality. You were very sweet – Really, I appreciate it."

"You're welcome, sweetie."

    Sandra smiled,

"Have a nice dream."

"You, too, Sandra," I replied smiling.

    She turned off the light, gave a little wave, and then closed the door slightly while leaving it partly open. I made myself comfortable and closed my eyes. The thoughts of Sandra eased my nerves – everything about her brings joy to my heart. Her presence made me feel calm and confident.

    Before I dozed off, I overheard Brooke and Talmar talking in the other room. No need to queue third person mode – I could hear them clearly. It sounded like they were discussing plans for tomorrow.

"Hey Doc, do you think we'll be able to walk around town with these guys? I'm nervous if someone sees them – They'll probably inform evil screw-head," said Brooke.

"Hmm... We'll just have to find a way to keep Alan and his two friends out of sight – Maybe roll them in a cart while they are covered by a cloth," said Talmar.

"...and where are we going to get a cart?"

"Perhaps the laundry bin down in the basement of this building?"

"We'll see by morning. Hey, when I retrieved these guys, Alan had this necklace on him."

"Really?"

"Yeah – Take a look at this.

"Fascinating – It has an interesting shape – Appears to look like an eye of some sort."

"Do you know what this is?"

"I'm afraid I don't."

"This is the Guardian Emblem – It is bestowed upon those who have demonstrated great acts of heroism – I'm sure a Guardian presented this to him but I'd be damned if he stole this..."

"Now Brooke, I doubt Alan would do that. I know you don't trust humans that much because of what happened in the past. Prejudice does not justify anything."

"Yeah – You're right."

"I do understand that when you were in human territory, people didn't take lightly to your heroic deeds. Unfortunately, humans are so primitive minded they can't accept differences in their society. That's why they are the only beings on this planet to cause conflict such as the wars they've fought. Most of their wars, as I have read, were due to territory and cultural differences. As you can see, that's why humans are primitive minded. They can't figure out better ways to solve their conflicts other than to kill off those who are different. Apparently, only a select few of the human species feel it is wise to handle conflicts using peace rather than war."

"You know it also kind of points back to our type. If you look now, half of this island went and invaded the human world and it only made things worse."

"Indeed – However, there is a way to make peace at the end of this situation. Surely, I believe it will end in spilling blood, sadly to say. One must fall for the others to stand."

"Let's hope the one to fall is that dirtbag at S. C. K. who screwed up everybody's life."

"The time will come, Brooke, when he will face justice."

"Yeah, let's try and shoot for it tomorrow."

"Brooke, before we turn in for the evening, I do recall reading a book on Anthronian races a while back. Since we're on the subject of unnecessary conflicts, I came across an article about the origin of the Najanians."

"*Really?*"

"I read they were humans at one point. They originated from Egypt and, as the text describes it, an anomalous sand storm blew through the desert and turned all inhabitants into half human, half reptilian beings. To be honest, I'm not a believer in myths and magic, however, I think it may have been a group of humans who underwent some sort of mutation giving them reptilian properties."

"If the story you read holds true, Doc, Najanians may be, in some way, actually human."

"Indeed – If they are, in fact, a race of humans, however..."

"Then... Holy Jesus..."

"It's something to think about, right?"

"Damn right – If the Najanians are a race of humans, then this war is more pointless than it already is."

"It most certainly is, my friend."

Both went off to their rooms and were done for the evening. At least I know where the Guardian Emblem went...

THE MASTERMIND
10

As morning came, I woke up feeling a lot better. The sun shined through the window, illuminating the room. I yawned and stretched. The bedroom door appeared to be open – probably someone had checked up on me. I heard a door open outside the room. Taking a small peek through the doorway, I noticed the bathroom door opening. In there, I saw Sandra wrapped up in a towel looking at herself in the mirror – she probably had just finished taking a shower. As she was about to exit the bathroom, I laid back down on the pillow, looking away.

I heard her walking over to a closet to get her clothes. She went back into the bathroom and closed the door. After about five minutes, she came out, walking in the direction of my room wearing a magenta-colored loin cloth and something resembling a sport bra. I pretended to be asleep so she wouldn't be surprised. She entered the room and I felt her petting my head. I opened my eyes and saw a pleasant smile on her face.

"Good morning, Alan. Did you get a good rest?" she asked.

"Yes, I did. Best sleep I had in a couple of days. How about you?"

"I got a good sleep, too. How are you feeling?"

"I feel a whole lot better, Sandra. Really, I thank you so much for your hospitality and the help from Brooke and Talmar."

"You're welcome – I'm glad you're feeling much better. All it takes is hope, happiness, and love."

Sandra placed her hand on my shoulder and smiled at me. She then asked me a question,

"Did you want breakfast? We have some good food to eat."

"What do you have available?"

"Talmar is about to cook some fish and eggs – We also have some fruit bowls, and I think we still have some cereal."

"I guess I'll have the fruit bowl – It's simple."

"Would you like to join us at the kitchen table?"

"I'd be delighted, Sandra – Thank you."

As I tried to get up, Sandra went and assisted me.

"Wait – Let me help you there."

She helped me sit up – fortunately, I had minimal complications. I wrapped the blanket around my waist as temporary clothing – wouldn't want Sandra to look at my bare tush...

"Okay, I'm going to walk you over to the bathroom so you can get dressed."

Sandra got my clothes and put them under her left arm. She walked me slowly to the bathroom. After we made it over there, I carefully sat down on the toilet seat. She placed my clothes on the sink and moved over to the door.

"Be careful when getting dressed. If you need anything, let me know, okay?"

"Thank you, Sandra."

Sandra patted my left shoulder, smiled, and turned to exit the bathroom, closing the door behind her. I removed the blanket from my waist and got dressed. Thankfully, I had no problems moving around. After getting my clothes on, I folded the blanket, left the bathroom, walked back to the bedroom, and placed the blanket down on the bed. I then proceeded into the kitchen and sat down at the table.

"Good morning, Alan. Feeling better, I heard," said Talmar.

"Indeed I am, Talmar. Seriously, I can't thank you guys enough for your help."

"You're very welcome."

"Oh, I almost forgot the fruit bowl. Let me get it for you," said Sandra.

Sandra went to the fridge and took out this nice sized fruit bowl.

"Here you go, Alan – Enjoy."

"Thank you, Sandra."

She gave me a fork and I opened the bowl. There was mango, pineapple, kiwi, and some berries. I dug in and it was delicious. Talmar had been cooking the fish and eggs – the aroma was strong, however, not bad. Soon after, Brooke entered the kitchen walking heavily. He appeared to be half asleep.

"Coffee..." moaned Brooke.

Brooke went over to the pantry and prepared some coffee. After he turned on the coffee maker, he walked into the living room and sat down in a chair.

"Does he always do that?" I asked.

"Yes, he does. After he has his coffee, he's his old self again," replied Talmar.

Sandra and Talmar chuckled at my question. I chuckled, too, seeing Brooke walking in like a zombie and wanting coffee, then walking out – weird, yet amusing.

"Alan, sorry to bother you while you're eating – Can you see if you can wake your friends?" asked Talmar.

"Sure – I'll see if I can."

I got up and walked into the living room. Marc and Lucky slept soundly on a large couch – a shame I'll have to wake them up. I went over to Marc first.

"Marc, wake up."

I shook him a little bit and then his eyes opened.

"Huh? Where are we?" asked Marc.

"Marc, we are in an apartment with three allied individuals who gave us hospitality and healed us back to normal health," I replied.

"I see – Looks like Lucky is still out cold."

"Hang on, I'll wake him up."

I went over to Lucky and tried to get him up.

"Lucky, wake up."

No reaction from him.

"Lucky, get your furry butt up."

With no response, I thought of something crazy that would get him up.

"Hey Lucky, we're in a place where we're being taken care of by some attractive Anthronian ladies. They want you to get up so they can give you a relaxing doggie massage."

Suddenly, Lucky awoke in excitement.

"Let me see, let me see – Hey, you lied to me."

"I had to get you up somehow."

"Where are we, anyway?"

"We are in an apartment with three allied individuals who gave us hospitality and healed us back to normal health."

"Please tell me it was three hot ladies."

"Lucky…"

"Alright, alright…"

"Anyway, they've invited you guys to come in the kitchen for breakfast."

As they were getting up, Talmar, Brooke, and Sandra came over to greet them. Marc felt uneasy.

"Good morning, gentlemen," said Talmar.

"Whoa…" said Marc.

"Please excuse my friend – He's not used to you yet."

"It's good to see these guys are awake," said Brooke.

I could tell Marc was freaking out.

"Where's the bathroom?" asked Marc.

"It's right over there," replied Talmar, pointing to the bathroom.

"Thank you."

Marc dashed into the bathroom and closed the door. In the meantime, I figured to introduce Lucky to the three.

"Marc probably got a little overwhelmed. Anyway, Lucky, I'd like you to meet Talmar, Brooke, and Sandra."

"It's nice to meet you all. Thanks for helping us."

"Much obliged, Lucky. Would you care to join us for breakfast?" asked Talmar.

"Sure – I am a little hungry."

We all went into the kitchen but before I could sit down and eat, I wanted to check up on Marc. I excused myself and went over to the bathroom door. Knocking three times, I asked,

"Marc, are you alright in there?"

"I'll be out in just a second," he replied.

He opened the door and faced me.

"Feeling better?"

"A little bit."

"Come inside, man. They want you to have something to eat."

"Okay."

I brought Marc into the kitchen and pulled out a seat for him. Brooke sat at the opposite end of the table from where I was sitting. On the right side of the table sat Talmar, sitting closer to Brooke, and then Sandra, who sat close to me at my end. Lucky sat opposite of Talmar. Marc sat to my left. I could tell he felt uneasy being at a table with humanoid beings.

"Marc, let me introduce you to these three. On the far side of the table is Brooke. On the right side is Talmar, and next to him, is Sandra."

"Hi," said Marc, nervously.

"Is there anything you would like for breakfast, Marc?" asked Talmar.

"Would you like a fruit bowl?" I added.

"Yeah, sure," replied Marc.

Sandra went over to the fridge to grab a fruit bowl. She gave Marc the bowl with a fork – he nodded thank you.

I knew he felt uncertain about our new friends. Regardless, Marc had to understand Sandra, Brooke, and Talmar may look odd but they are allies. He ate silently, not looking up at all. During this time, Brooke sipped his coffee and Talmar served the fish and eggs. Lucky had some eggs and Sandra had a little bit of both. I finished the fruit bowl and waited until everyone else finished.

"Did you enjoy the fruit, Alan?" asked Sandra.

"Yes, it was quite refreshing – Thank you."

On the table down near Brooke, I saw a newspaper. I figured while I wait, I can look at it.

"Brooke, may I look at the newspaper please?"

"Sure, there's not much good news, but here you go."

Brooke slid the paper down to me and I looked at the cover. The front page said, "President gives OK to invade." I opened the paper and turned the pages to find the main information. While reading the article, I noticed the Anthronian President wasn't the mastermind – he worked *with* the mastermind. As I read on, I found the name of the one who plotted the mayhem. His name was Mantor. Unfortunately, there was no picture of him.

"Find anything interesting, Al?" asked Lucky.

"Yeah, I found the name of the mastermind."

"What's his name?"

"His name is Mantor," Talmar answered.

"I call him evil screw-head," Brooke added.

"Mantor? His name sounds more like man whore," said Lucky.

We all laughed over Lucky's comment. Brooke, especially, laughed hysterically.

"Oh my God, that was good," said Brooke.

"Apparently, he is the one we need to confront," said Marc.

"Exactly – We need to locate his lair and definitely have a long talk with him," I said.

"Hate to be a 'buzz kill' for you fellows, but talking to Mantor is literally impossible," said Talmar.

"How come?" asked Lucky.

"Once Mantor sees the presence of humans, he shoots first, and then asks questions," said Brooke.

"Mantor is a horrible man – Death is nothing to him – He even…" said Sandra, and then pausing.

She seemed hurt about thinking of something. Her eyes became glassy and then hung her head.

"Can you guys excuse me for a moment, I'm sorry."

Sandra got up and went to her room – silence filled the kitchen.

"Oh dear," said Talmar.

"Is everything alright?" I asked.

Brooke and Talmar seemed concerned to see Sandra upset.

"Do you want to tell them?" Brooke asked Talmar.

"Very well – When Sandra was the age of seven, her father had been working for Mantor's company, S. C. Kharaab, Corp. One evening, Mantor came by the house. Sandra's father told her to head upstairs. Eventually, an argument broke out causing Mantor to become enraged. Taking out a hand-held weapon, he shot her parents. Sandra, sadly, witnessed the crime. Mantor attempted to go after her. Sandra fled the scene and ran to Brooke's house. From there, Brooke's parents contacted the police but by the time they did arrive, everything was cleaned up – No evidence what so ever. The police investigated the suspicions surrounding Mantor, however, they could not convict him and the case had been dropped."

"Damn," commented Lucky.

"That's horrible," said Marc.

"Do you mind if I go and check on Sandra?" I asked.

"By all means, Alan. I do feel she would be happy to see you," replied Talmar.

I excused myself and went to Sandra's room – I knocked on her door.

"Who is it?" she asked.

"Alan," I replied.

"You can come in."

I entered and saw Sandra lying sideways on her bed facing away from the door. I could tell the memory of her horrible experience really hurt her inside.

"Are you alright, Sandra?"

"So-so – I'm sorry I'm like this."

"It's okay – It's alright to feel sad – We all have a lot of moments where we remember something that makes us hurt inside."

I went over to sit down on her bed – I put my hand on her left shoulder.

"I know what it's like to lose a loved one. For one thing, my father passed away a year ago."

"How did he die?" asked Sandra.

"Well, to make a long story short, one day, I came home from school and found my father on the floor at the base of the stairway – I initially thought he fell down the stairs and hurt himself badly – I went over to him and asked him what happened. The response I got was slurred speech – I quickly ran over to the phone and dialed nine-one-one. Within five to seven minutes, the rescue team arrived – When they brought my father to the hospital, one of the responders told me my father suffered a serious stroke."

I paused for a moment – thinking back on the memory started to take its toll on me.

"My father stayed in the hospital for three weeks. During that time, his body deteriorated and was slowly dying. On the evening of February fifteenth, the hospital called my house and informed my mother and me that my father had passed away."

I felt some tears coming but I held them back. Sandra sat up and turned to me. I could sense her concern.

"That must have been horrible," she said.

"I literally went to Hell that day."

I looked down at the floor, re-envisioning the horrors I saw.

"Are *you* okay?" she asked.

"Yeah – I'm okay."

I turned to Sandra,

"Are you doing alright?" I asked.

"A little better."

"You know what you need? You need a big hug – Whenever I feel down, my mom always hugs me."

Sandra smiled and I gave her a big hug. It felt good for me, too. While she embraced me, I felt a lot better – she was a good hugger. After our embrace, I asked,

"Do you feel much better?"

"I do – I feel much better," she replied, smiling.

"Good."

"Thank you."

Sandra rested her hand on the side of my face and gazed at me with loving eyes. We stared at each other for a minute longer. I then invited her to come back into the kitchen.

"Come, Sandra, let's head back inside, okay?"

Sandra smiled and nodded. We exited her room and went back to the kitchen.

"Feeling better?" asked Talmar.

"I feel a lot better, thank you," replied Sandra.

Brooke gave me thumbs up signifying he appreciated my help. I nodded in acknowledgment.

"After we're done with breakfast, we'll get down to what we need to do today," said Brooke.

After everyone finished, we all went into the living room and sat down. Brooke stood up in front of all of us.

"Okay, today we need to infiltrate Mantor's mansion," started Brooke, "There's a hidden path to the south. It's a narrow road leading up a hill and I'm not sure if it will be heavily guarded or not – We should prepare for anything."

"Just in case we face some serious combat, Marc and I should get down to adjusting a couple of things with our armor," I said.

"Do you have a toolbox we can use?" asked Marc.

"Yeah, I have one in my room – I'll show you," said Brooke.

Brooke brought us to his room and took out a toolbox. It had just enough tools to help us modify the armor.

"Let us know when you're done. We got to be out of here ASAP," said Brooke.

Marc and I laid our armor out and looked at it for a moment.

"I think we should remove the cups," I said.

"Yeah, those are so uncomfortable – Let's definitely get rid of those."

"Hey guys, since you're cutting away some metal, can I use the extra pieces to construct armor for myself?" asked Lucky.

"I see why not," I replied.

Marc and I cut away some excess metal not needed anymore. During this time, Lucky proceeded to build a small metal vest for himself. Fifteen minutes had passed and we made a lot of progress. Sandra dropped by to see how we were doing.

"Hey guys, did you want anything to drink?"

"Nah, I'm okay," answered Lucky.

"No thank you, I'm not really thirsty," answered Marc.

"No thank you, Sandra. I'm okay for the moment."

"So, how are you guys doing?" she asked.

"We're just about done," I replied.

I showed Sandra the modifications and showed what Lucky made with the spare metal. Sandra seemed quite impressed.

"Not bad, guys."

"Hopefully, these modifications are worth it," I said.

Sandra smiled back at me in response.

"If you guys need anything, let me know."

"You got it," I replied, with a smile.

Sandra walked away – Lucky started nudging me with his elbow.

"Hey Al, I think she's checkin' you out – She be smiling and gazing at you – She wants you, man."

"Lucky, come on, she's not even human. Why would she have an interest in Alan?"

"It doesn't matter my brutha – Let me explain it to you in another way," started Lucky, "When a man loves a woman…"

Lucky started to sing out loud – Marc and I had to shush him to make him stop.

"Sorry, got a little carried away. But seriously, man, I can sense she really likes you. So far, you been treating her right and she's getting all flattered. Man, I can see you two together. Plus with a nice booty like that…"

"Okay, Lucky, I think it's time to give it a rest," said Marc.

"She is very kind and has a sweet personality – She's just so wonderful," I said.

"Yeah, boy, I see those loving eyes. You're getting that feeling now, eh?"

"Can we concentrate on finishing up please?" Marc implored.

We dropped the subject and finished up. Lucky, I could tell, saw Sandra and I had something going on. Hopefully, Lucky wouldn't get carried away with it but knowing him… enough said.

Marc, Lucky, and I walked back into the living room with our armor. We got our gear on and got ready. Brooke brought in our weapons.

"Okay, boys, here are your guns. Oh, Al, don't forget this…"

Brooke tossed me the Guardian Emblem.

"Thank you. Hey Brooke, do you know anything about this?"

"Yeah – The Guardian Emblem is a symbol of honor – It is bestowed upon those who have done incredible acts of heroism. It also symbolizes truth, justice, and hope. Legend has it, a group of heroes, centuries ago, band together to take on a powerful evil. Through their teamwork, they conquered the evil force and created an age of peace. They were called The Guardians and each wore the eye shaped emblem."

Brooke pulled out another Guardian Emblem from a pouch he had on him.

"My dad gave me this. It has been passed down from generation to generation. He told me this story. How did you come by yours?"

"A female gargoyle gave it to me a couple of nights ago."

"Luna."

"The one with blue skin and white hair?" I asked.

"Yep – Her family tree goes way back – She had great grandparents who were Guardians."

"Brooke, aren't one of your past relatives a Guardian?" asked Sandra.

"Yeah."

"So, that means she's your cousin?" asked Lucky.

"Second cousin, actually."

"Is she hot?" asked Lucky.

Brooke looked at Lucky and shook his head in derision.

"You want me to shut up?"

Brooke nodded yes.

"Alright, alright – I'll shut up – Let's proceed with the mission."

"Follow me," Brooke ordered.

I placed the necklace around my neck, hiding the emblem in my shirt. We left the apartment and carefully walked down the stairway to the lobby. Brooke went ahead to make sure the coast was clear.

"Alright, I'm going to see what it's like outside," said Brooke.

He opened the entrance door and peeked out. After a moment, he gave the okay. Carefully walking outside, we saw a barren city – the streets empty and quiet. No one was around.

"Where is everyone?" asked Sandra.

"This is quite odd," said Talmar.

"Man, this place is a ghost town," I said.

"Hey, look at that poster. Maybe that's why it's so quiet around here," said Marc, pointing to a poster on a wall.

We all looked at the poster and it said there was an urgent town meeting.

"Heh, a town meeting? Our president must have literally flipped his lid," said Brooke.

"I say we take advantage of the situation and proceed to the hidden path pronto," said Lucky.

Marc, Lucky, and I followed the three up the road to a path surrounded by trees. A narrow dirt road can be seen leading up a hill.

"Okay, let's go," said Brooke.

Brooke led the way – we kept our eyes open for any guards patrolling the area. On our way, we came across an abandoned golf cart. No guards appeared to be around so we decided to take the vehicle.

"Are you thinking what I'm thinking?" asked Lucky.

"My thoughts exactly," said Brooke.

We all got in the golf cart unit – six people could fit in it. Lucky and Marc sat on a bench in the back. Brooke took the wheel up front and Talmar sat next to him. I was in the back seat with Sandra.

It took a few minutes to approach Mantor's mansion. While looking at the place, it was a fairly large property covering at least fifteen thousand square feet. Brooke carefully drove up next to the garage entrance on the side. We noticed an adjacent security door and went over to it. The door was locked.

"There must be a way in," said Brooke.

"Is that a code lock on there?" asked Lucky.

"Yeah."

"Let me try and hack it."

Lucky proceeded to attach a pair of wires from his device to the lock. Within a matter of seconds, the lock was disengaged.

"Brilliant – Good work, Lucky," said Talmar.

We entered the garage and it was dimly lit. Marc, Lucky, and I got our weapons ready. Suddenly, the lights went out. Only a spotlight shined above – darkness surrounded us.

"I have a bad feeling about this," said Talmar.

"Keep your eyes peeled and your ears perked," I ordered.

"I think it would be hard for Sandra and Talmar to have perked ears, Al," started Lucky, "Since, you know, they don't have ears like you and me."

"Not the best time for jokes, Luck."

The lights dimmed on a bit, illuminating the garage slightly. We started hearing deep growling and heavy footsteps in the distance. Looking around, I noticed a large figure approaching. The entity had to be at least between eight and ten feet tall, had a built physique, and seemed like an overgrown lizard man. As the creature got close to us, it paused. Other entities appeared to populate the area. All of a sudden, a sinister British voice appeared on a loud speaker.

"Welcome – You all must be the heroes – I've been expecting you."

"That's him," said Sandra.

"Still sounds the same the last we encountered him," added Talmar.

"Now come along quietly and drop your weapons. If you fail to comply, I'll order my men to open fire."

The lights dimmed on little more and we got a clear look at our opponents. The large creature was a T-Rex man – certainly not a guy to mess with.

"A big bulky dude with metal underwear? Hey man whore, if you want to scare us, at least dress him up in something that makes him scary not something that's going to embarrass the guy," said Lucky.

Marc, Lucky, and I threw our weapons on the ground and complied. There was no way we could take on several armed guards and a T-Rex man.

The guards brought us to an elevator, heading downward. The descent felt like a ride into Hell. After the elevator stopped, the guards brought us to a room split by a bulletproof sheet of glass. We all sat down on a bench and waited.

"The Master will see you shortly," said the guard.

The guard left and locked the door.

"Well, this sucks," said Marc.

After a minute passed, the door on the opposite side opened. I felt my blood run cold. Mantor walked in and turned to us with a stern, evil look. He was a Najanian with blood red eyes, stood about six feet tall, wore a red loin cloth, and had this creepy, yet fascinating, tattoo of a scarab on the left side of his chest.

"Welcome – How nice it is for you all to drop in. May I ask what you are doing, especially with these humans and… dog?"

"For your information, we're coming to stop your evil plan and what you're going to do to the humans," answered Sandra.

"Ah, Sandra… How long has it been?"

Sandra gave a dirty look in return while Mantor gave a sinister smile.

"I guess you're still mad at me for killing your... mommy and daddy was it?"

"Go to Hell you bastard – You leave her alone – For the Hell you put her through, I should rip your head off and shove it up your ass," exclaimed Brooke.

Brooke approached the glass aggressively – Talmar got up and put his hand on his shoulder to keep him at ease. They both sat back down. Mantor gave an arrogant smirk.

"Really, Mister Stone? I'm curious, where did you find these humans and... dog thing?"

"I'm a canine humanoid, dumb ass," said Lucky.

"Whatever..."

"We found these humans after your security team in the city came across them and almost killed them," Talmar answered.

"Ah, these three must be a part of the ones we took in yesterday. I can figure the one wearing red is the leader, are you not?"

Mantor stared at me with his evil eyes. I felt a little intimidated but I found the strength to reply.

"Yes, I am. How did you know?"

"I was able to get some information out of your friends when we brought them in."

"Are they okay?"

"For now, they are."

"Don't you dare hurt them," exclaimed Marc.

"Marc, at ease," I said while trying to keep him cool.

"Hm hm hm... What is your name red warrior?"

"My name is Alan."

"I assume Sandra and her friends told you all about me?"

"Question – Why did you invade the world and where are you taking everyone?"

"I invaded for many reasons. You should have some idea of what those reasons may be."

"How would we know?" asked Marc.

"Let me explain in detail, shall I? I'm bringing you humans here so I can put all of you into slavery," started Mantor, "It's time that *we* have a say in things rather than being harassed by *your* kind. Some told me to negotiate with your world leaders but I knew humans never negotiate – They take their weapons and use it against us."

"Brutha, calm down – We get how you feel," said Lucky.

"Do you realize how many lives were destroyed? My team and I had to walk through Hell to get here," I said with anger.

"Does it look like I care?"

"Apparently not," I replied.

"Exactly."

Mantor stared at me with such a sinister look. I could tell he wanted me dead. It looked like he wanted to come through the glass and kill me on the spot.

"Are death and destruction all you care about?" asked Sandra.

"I pity the weak – Humans are weak – Therefore they must submit to me. For thousands of years, humans have exiled us to this bloody island. It is time for a change."

Mantor looked at me with his villainous eyes.

"By the way, I heard reports of you playing hero on several roads around a town called Levittown. I heard you held off a large group of my minions while protecting your friends."

"I was rescuing my friend's sister. She was defenseless."

"Yeah, and I thank him for that," Marc added.

"Really – Why do you feel it is necessary to play hero, human? Do you think you can actually win? One way or another, your blood will spill and I can tell you now you will not live long. I am surprised you've made it this far. Tomorrow, you will be executed. I will make sure every last drop of blood comes out of you."

I could tell Mantor meant every bit of that – he wasn't bluffing.

"What about my friends? What are you going to do to them?" I asked.

"I will decide who will be of service to me – I've already decided who will be my own personal slaves."

"You do anything to my brother, I'll whoop yo ass," exclaimed Lucky.

"Really? I doubt you'll be able to."

"We'll see who goin' get smoked, bitch."

"As for you Sandra, you will be executed at the same time with the human. I've waited a long time to kill you and soon you will join your departed parents."

"You won't get away with this, Mantor," exclaimed Sandra.

"Once I get out, your ass is mine," exclaimed Brooke.

"We'll see about that Mister Stone. As for the rest of you, I'll let you rot in the brig. Of course, I do want to have an extended chat with you, *Alan*."

His blood red eyes felt like death looking straight at me. I knew the conversation wasn't going to be pleasant.

"You're a monster, you know that? Sooner or later, the human race will rise against you," exclaimed Marc.

Mantor chuckled and summoned a few guards. He ordered one to take me to the interrogation room. As we were brought out, my buddies went one way, while I went another. Sandra looked back at me and mouthed my name – she looked distraught. I know she did not want me to suffer.

The guard brought me to a dimly lit room, pushed me up against the wall, and shackled my wrists and ankles.

After the guard left, a sinister looking female Najanian appeared in the doorway. She wore tight-fitting purple apparel. For her upper body, she wore a wraparound loin cloth and for her lower body, she wore a bikini-like bottom. She, too, had jewelry – two sets of arm cuffs, two bracelets on both her wrists and an ankle bracelet on her right ankle. After a moment, she began to walk towards me.

"Hello, human. My hubby will be in shortly. In the meantime, I will get started interrogating you."

She spoke with a snobbish tone.

"Why did you come here?"

"I came here with my friends to get to the bottom of why this island invaded our town and the rest of the world."

"So, you thought playing hero would save your species?"

She came closer while looking at me with a stern look. Cupping my chin, she gave a sly smile.

"In a way, this is quite amusing – Ha, pathetic mammal."

Anger built up inside of me. If I wasn't chained to the wall, I'd bop her one.

"For a scrawny nothing, I doubt you'd ever be anything great – On the other hand, you can be a nice tender snack," she said, licking her lips.

She moved closer to me. Moving to the right side of my face, she grasped my chin tightly.

"I can smell your fear… and I can taste it…"

The door opened – Mantor entered.

"Hello, Sphinx, I'll take care of the human from here."

"Can I stay and watch? I won't interfere, dear."

"Very well."

Mantor walked over to me. Deep within, I could see hatred and torment. Something made him snap.

"Alright, Alan, I'll be asking you a few questions and then I'll throw you back in the brig."

"Okay."

"Question one – What made you think you could thwart my plans?"

"Hey, I didn't expect this part to occur. I thought once we got here, we would find our way to you and have a peaceful talk."

"Hm hm hm... You wanted to speak to me peacefully? I think Sandra and her friends could have told you I don't do that."

"Yeah, I could see."

I felt nervous about Mantor. He definitely, without a doubt, was an egotistical, power-hungry psychopath.

"Question two – How were you able to beat most of my minions? Just a moment ago, I received word the Clymerian Queen and my dragon were found dead. I wouldn't be surprised if you and your friends had anything to do with it."

"Yeah – We did have something to do with that."

"How is that possible?" Mantor exclaimed.

"We had..."

"Wait a second – What's that you have around your neck?" said Mantor, cutting me off.

Mantor approached me and pulled out the Guardian Emblem.

"Where did you get this?"

"Why do you ask?"

"Where did you get this?" he raised his voice.

"A female gargoyle gave it to me."

"Hmm... I see..."

Mantor looked at me and then back at the emblem. It's as if he knew what it meant. He let it drop back to my chest and resumed asking me questions.

"Question three – Is there something going on between you and Sandra? I've noticed she seemed quite concerned about you."

"Something, such as like a friend?"

"No, my dear boy – Not like a friend – I'm talking about relationship wise."

"Oh – No, I don't believe it's that. If you meant friendship wise, then that would be a yes."

Mantor didn't seem amused with my answer. It's like he sensed Sandra and I did have something going on – our little connection in other words.

"Mantor, if I may, let me relieve you from your questions and let me ask one. Why did you kill Sandra's parents?"

Mantor turned and looked at me with intent to kill. That stoic, sinister stare made my blood run cold.

"I had good reason – I suggest you don't ask me again."

"Still, is killing really necessary? You know, I handle everything with words and things turn out a whole lot better, if you ask me."

"Words are for fools, human. It's the same reason why I didn't bother negotiating with your world leaders. War gets the job done, boy."

"Why do you hate humans so much?"

"Stop asking questions."

"Is it something that happened to you in the past?"

"Silence."

"I want to know so I can try and help you."

Mantor grabbed my neck and held me against the wall – he moved closer, his eyes fixated on me.

"Help? I don't need any help – Especially from a human cretin like you."

I remained silent until he moved away and released my neck.

"Look, I'm sorry if I brought back a bad memory but seriously, you have a ton of anger inside you. You have to learn to let the past go."

"I'm not going to discuss with you any further about my life."

Something made this guy evil. One way or another I will attempt to extract it from him – hopefully, without getting killed in the process.

"I have one final question for you – Why do you do good deeds? I received reports of you sacrificing yourself for your friends and, obviously, you're sacrificing yourself for the human species. Why not save yourself? Why would you want to put your life on the line for people who would most likely leave you to die?"

"Because it's the right thing to do. As many have seen, I do good things. My mother's kind nature taught me the difference between right and wrong. I help people because I want to. People need a hero to guide them through the darkness – Someone who can give them hope."

"There is no hope – You can't save everyone, Alan, and eventually heroes fall. You don't realize with all the effort you put in, you'll never win in the end."

"Heroes never fall for good – We will always rise up again like a Phoenix from the ashes."

"We will see – I am done asking you questions. To remind you, you will be executed with Sandra tomorrow. Soon she will join her parents and there's nothing you can do about it."

He ordered a guard to throw me into the brig. I had to think hard about how we're getting out of this situation... alive. The guard unshackled me and brought me out of the room while Mantor and Sphinx watched.

BUSTIN' OUT
II

A Minotaur guard escorted me to the prison area and another guard opened the cell door. The Minotaur threw me into the cell with Marc and Sandra. My back hit the wall and I dropped to the floor.

"And stay in there until you rot, human," exclaimed the Minotaur.

Sandra and Marc helped me up and moved me over to one of the prison beds.

"Holy crap," said Marc.

"That hurt," I said, in agony.

"Oh, my," Sandra added.

"Al, is that you?" asked Lucky.

Lucky came up to a barred window, overlooking the neighboring cell – he was happy to see me alive.

"You okay, man?"

"Hangin' in there, Luck – Who's with you?"

"It's me, Roller, Brooke, and Talmar – The rest of your buddies are in the next three cells."

I acknowledged Lucky – Sandra sat beside me. I began to think about what Mantor had said to me.

"I'm assuming you did not have a good conversation with Mantor, right?" asked Marc.

"Nope, it was not a good conversation at all. We talked and now I understand what he said."

"What did he say?" asked Sandra.

"He told me that I can't save everyone, and in the end, I'll never win. If I think back to my father, I saved him yet he still died."

"Alan, it wasn't your fault for your father's death. You did what a true hero would do in the face of something so horrible. You had no control over the outcome. Stop blaming yourself," said Marc.

I could hear Jason and Rebekah arguing in the neighboring cells. Laura and Charles tried easing the dispute.

"Guys – Fighting with each other won't get us out of here," said Laura.

"Yeah – So, sit down, shut up, and cool it," said Charles.

While all this was going on, Sandra held me close to her. Brooke popped in through the neighboring bars.

"Hey Al, can you tell your buddies to quiet down? If you want, I'll quiet them for you," asked Brooke.

I gave Brooke the okay to do so. Sandra rested her head on my shoulder. Marc observed the interaction I was having with her. He seemed both confused and fascinated.

"Hey, friends of Alan – Pipe down. We're trying to think of a way out of here," shouted Brooke.

"Who the hell are you?" asked Rebekah, aggressively.

"Let me tell you sweet cheeks, we're on your side – Let's put our heads together so we can think of a way to bust out."

Lucky came up to the bars and looked through.

"How's big Al?" asked Lucky.

"He's doing fine. There must be a way to get these doors open. Got any ideas, Luck?" asked Marc.

"I'll see if I can hack through the door but it seems too tough to get to the control panel. I tried to connect wirelessly but for some reason, I can't tap into it."

"Alan, are you able to think of something?" asked Sandra.

"I can't really think now – I feel I've let everyone down – I don't know if I can do it."

"Yes, you can, Alan. The day when you found your father on the floor, you called for help – You knew what to do and you thought of it fast – You did what you could do for him. I know, deep within, you have the solution to this situation."

Sandra put her hand on the side of my face – she moved closer to me.

"Alan, if you were able to save your friends before, I know you can do it again. If your dad was still alive today, he'd be proud of you for your achievements. I'm proud of you for not only being my friend but for being a wonderful guy. You have a strong heart, Alan. Listen to what it's telling you – Follow it – I believe in you – I know you can do it."

Sandra put her hand on my chest over my heart. I pulled out the Guardian Emblem and looked at it. The gargoyle gave it to me because she believed in me – Sandra believed in me – I had to believe in me. I put my hand on Sandra's and said confidently,

"You keep this heart beating, I'll give you all the plans you want – I'll see what I can do."

Sandra smiled in response. Looking at the cell door, I noticed a set of bars on each side of it. I remembered the guard accessed a security console adjacent to the prison cell. Suddenly, it hit me,

"I have an idea," I said.

I went over to the barred window and looked through into the neighboring cell with Brooke, Lucky, Roller, and Talmar.

"Brooke, come here for a second."

"What's up?"

"Can you try and pull apart the bars adjacent to the cell door? I think you have enough strength to do that."

"I'll give it a shot. What's your idea?"

"If you can pull them apart far enough, Lucky can squeeze through and access the security console outside the cell door."

"Clever idea, Al," Lucky commented.

"Let's do this," said Brooke.

Brooke went over to the bars and pulled with all his might – It looked promising...

"Luck, see if you can fit through," I said.

Lucky hopped up and tried squeezing through the opening.

"Man, I feel like a baby coming out of a birth canal."

"Push, dude," said Roller.

Lucky pushed himself through and landed on the floor.

"Yo, Bro, I need you here, too. I'm too short to reach the console."

Roller hopped up and squeezed through the opening with little issue.

"Okay, lift me up on your shoulders while I do this."

"Make it quick, dude. I don't know how long I can hold ya."

Roller lifted Lucky up to the console. He began tinkering with it until both cell doors opened.

"Heh, child's play."

"Great work, Luck," I said.

Marc, Sandra, and I exited our cell and went over to the other doors to open them. After opening the last cell door, we all regrouped in the hallway.

"Okay guys, we need to find substantial weaponry before we can proceed," I said.

"Al, there's a security office down at the end of the hall," said Marc.

"Let's role."

We made our way down to the security office. Brooke volunteered to go in and take care of the guards. We heard them getting beaten up and thrown around. Brooke came out and gave the okay.

"Alright everyone, load up," I ordered.

We entered the office, grabbed our guns, and got ready. Some took an assault rifle called the C2AR. Evan certainly liked the gun most of all. Bill and Mike also took the C2AR as their primary weapon. It ran on ten-millimeter ammunition and each mag contained sixty bullets. Lucky and Roller loaded up with Uzis and some extra mags. We took plenty of ammo and were ready to face Mantor. Sandra, Talmar, and Brooke didn't take weapons due to small reasons. First, they didn't know how to use guns and second, Brooke *is* a weapon. We walked out of the office and went down to the brig exit.

Once we got there, the doors opened and there stood two guards. Evan and Charles fired their weapons and took them down with ease.

"Booya – Take that to the bank," said Charles.

"Area clear," said Evan.

"Let's move out," I ordered.

"Which way is the exit?" asked Lucky.

"We were brought in that way," said Mike, pointing down the hallway corridor.

"Guys, guards are coming from that direction," said Charles.

"Damn, we're blocked," said Evan.

"There's got to be another way," I said.

"If we can find an alternate route, we may be able to get around them," said Chris.

"Let's go this way guys," said Mike.

"Let's go," Charles added.

THE PLANS
12

We ran down the hall with Mike leading the way. As we approached another hallway, a few guards came around prepared to open fire. Charles fired a couple of shots from his pistols at the guards' knees, wounding them. He then used some of his martial arts on one of them and took him down. Evan hit the other one with the base of the C2AR, knocking him out cold.

"Excellent work — Let's keep moving," I ordered.

We took the hallway the guards came down. At the end of the path, a large metal door blocked our way. A console, to enter an access code, hung on the wall. Lucky went over to try and decipher it. A few seemed quite nervous about the situation.

"Great — A dead end," said Rebekah.

"This sucks," Jason added.

"What do we do?" asked Laura.

"Let me see if I can bash through it," said Brooke.

Brooke punched the door a few times but no luck. He didn't even leave a dent.

"Dammit — Man, this door must be like a few inches of steel."

"Hey guys, I think we might be able to get the door open. I may need some time to hack the console, though," said Lucky.

"Are you sure you're able to do it, Luck?" I asked.

"Sure I can — Just buy me some time."

"Al, we got company," said Evan.

"From both ways," Charles added.

"Shoot – Brooke, see if you can rip these metal plates off the wall and put them in the floor standing up right. We need shields – We may encounter heavy firepower."

"You got it."

"Evan and Charles, hold your position up front," I ordered.

"Roger."

"Chris, Bill, and Mike – Hold a position behind those two."

"Got it."

"Rebekah, take right side – Laura, take left side."

"Got it."

"Jason, cover behind Chris, Bill, and Mike."

"Affirmative."

"Talmar, stand by the door and stay low."

"Got it."

"Sandra and Roller, cover Lucky."

"Roger."

"Brooke, hold position behind Jason."

"I'm on it."

"Marc, cover door."

"Standing by."

"Lucky, do your thing – We've got your back."

We could hear the guards approaching. This will be our first heavy gun fight out of the whole adventure. Hopefully, we will be able to take down the guards with ease. I hope I made the right choice in team member placement. This was a game of chess with guns.

"Here they come," said Charles.

I tensed up – we had to cover Lucky and make sure he gets the door open. In a way, it felt like the assault campaign in one of my favorite games. One team assaults the objective, while the other team defends the objective. We were on defense.

"Incoming," shouted Evan.

The guards came around with force and fired their weapons at us. Evan, Charles, Chris, Bill, Mike, and Brooke took down a good amount with only a few slipping by them. Bullets flew everywhere – it felt like a war zone.

"Luck, how's the hacking?" I asked.

"Just one more minute," he replied.

"We're taking heavy fire – I don't know how much longer we can take," said Marc.

"We're gonna get through this – Just hang in there."

Within a few seconds, Lucky had just completed cracking the code on the door console.

"Finished," shouted Lucky.

"Marc and Roller, secure the door and make sure we don't have company on the other side," I ordered.

"Affirmative."

They positioned themselves and got ready to take on any hostiles on the other side of the door. Roller took a peek under to see if it was safe. He gave the thumbs-up to indicate a clear path. Once the door got high enough, I called out to everyone,

"Guys, fall back – Door is open."

We all ran through the doorway while Evan and Charles held off remaining guards.

"Lucky, shut the door," I ordered.

"You got it."

He managed to shut the door remotely. After the door finally closed, we relaxed for a moment. All of us were out of breath and some suffered minor injuries.

"Man, that was tough," said Charles.

"Damn, man – That was some crazy crap," said Evan.

"Is everyone okay?" I asked.

Everybody nodded yes. They were so exhausted they couldn't speak.

"Sorry it took long but their encryption program was tough. My device has never come across a system like that," said Lucky.

"Thankfully, it cracked the code, dude," said Roller.

"Okay, guys, let's proceed onward," I ordered.

We came to a tall door on the left side of the hall. A sign hung on it saying "Computer Lab." The door had a little window on the top portion of it. I asked Brooke if he could peer through it since I wasn't tall enough to reach the window.

"Brooke, can you look through the window and see what's inside?"

"Sure."

He took a peek and looked briefly.

"So, what did you see?" asked Lucky.

"A huge computer room with several occupants standing around."

"We need to access a computer – Information on Mantor's plans must be in there," said Marc.

"Lucky, can that device of yours wirelessly connect to their computer in there?" asked Bill.

"Yeah."

"Can you connect to the computer at this moment?"

"Sure, I can."

Lucky connected to the computer in the room. Something told me Bill had this interesting and whacky idea.

"Okay, what's your idea?"

"I have a flash drive containing a video file I made to fool Mikey D. on his computer when he opened his email."

"Dude, don't remind me. You made me send my computer to a repair shop and I wasted fifty bucks on nothing," said Mike, angrily.

"Sorry, Mike, I'll repay you… eventually. Anyway, can this flash drive plug into your device?"

"Yeah, I got a port for it."

Lucky took the flash drive from Bill and plugged it in. He opened the file and prepared to send it to the computer in the room.

"Okay, let's hope this works," said Lucky, pressing the transmit button.

The file was sent to the main computer. We got a glimpse of it on Lucky's device. Bill created a little video, when opened, popped up and simulated a virus infecting the computer. It showed Bill's face floating around the screen. His face moved to one side and then a picture of a hard drive appeared. He then fired lasers from his eyes at the hard drive and text appeared saying "Hard Drive has been erased." Next, Bill's face flew to the center of the screen and said the computer will self-destruct in thirty seconds.

"Hey guys, I think it's working," said Brooke.

We started hearing the occupants inside becoming worried. Apparently, they were trying to figure out how to clear the fake virus. Then we heard one of them speak.

"Everyone please evacuate – This system has gone berserk. Let's head out through the emergency exit in a calm fashion," said one of the operators.

Brooke informed us the room had been cleared out. We carefully entered the room and saw the ending of Bill's silly little prank video. In the end, Bill says "Gonna blow up your face!" then Bill's face explodes. After the conclusion of the video, it rebooted the system. Upon boot up, it went to the main log on screen.

Marc sat down in the chair and attempted to log on. He pulled out a flash drive containing a separate operating system which would allow him to bypass the password and still access hard drive information. He placed the flash drive into the computer's USB port and rebooted the system. Then, he accessed the flash drive through the troubleshoot screen and proceeded to peruse through the data on the hard drive.

"Okay guys, I'm able to get through. Just keep a look out for any guards."

"Roger that," I replied.

While Marc browsed Mantor's main computer, I asked Chris, Bill, and Mike to take care of some tasks,

"Bill, check security cams and keep an eye out for opposition."

"I'm on it."

"Chris, see if you can pull up a floor plan of this place on another computer and print it out."

"Okay."

"Mike, stick with Chris because I need you to navigate our way out of here."

"Got it."

For everyone else, I told them to be on standby. I moved over to Marc and looked at the monitor.

"Al, I found Mantor's plans – It's this file right here plus a few others within the same folder."

"Let's take a look."

"Okay, here is what the plans say," started Marc, "Step one – Send cruisers full of troops and cages to all parts of the world. Step two – Capture every last human and destroy those who resist with violence. Step three – Secure humans at specified locations and wait for further orders from the Clymerian Embassy. Step four – Enslave human kind and take over human territory."

"Well, I think we have already figured that out. We saw everything back at home. They came in large ships, they attacked everywhere, did tremendous destruction, and we saw a portion of the human population being brought here," I said.

"We have to make sure he doesn't complete the last step," said Sandra.

"Wait, I found some other info. There's one more plan he has."

"Let's take a look," I said.

Marc tried opening the document but it required a password. Above the password field, there was a string of text.

"People have judged me – I sit with other misfits – We sit, forever untouched – Where am I?" I read aloud.

"Is that a riddle?" asked Jason.

"I believe it is – Do you know what the answer is, J?" I asked.

Jason looked at the riddle, closed his eyes, and thought deeply. After a moment, he came to an epiphany.

"I got it."

Jason whispered the answer into Marc's ear. He typed it in and it worked.

"Hold on – What's the answer?" asked Lucky.

"I think we should let the folks at home have a shot at it," said Jason.

"Yeah – Let's see if you guys can figure it out at home…" I said.

"Guys, sorry to interrupt your fourth wall breaking, but take a look at this…" said Marc.

The file contained plans about an army of special creatures supervising the slaves.

"Guys, there are further specs on these creatures. Holy crap…" started Marc.

"What it is?" I asked.

"Look at what this says."

"Genetically engineered lizard men – Code name: BIO-LM," I read aloud.

"There are two other files in the genetics folder that are encrypted. I don't have time to decrypt them but I'll copy these to my other flash drive just so we have some evidence," said Marc.

"Guys, we got some guards coming. I just saw them on camera one," said Bill.

"Okay – Marc, do you have all necessary info?" I asked.

"Got all that I needed."

"Good – Proceed through the emergency exit. Chris, do you have a map printed out?"

"Got it right here."

"Okay – Mike, take a look at it and figure a way out of here."

"Roger."

After we left the room, Brooke took a metal pipe and wrapped it around the handles to seal it. While walking along the emergency passage, we found our way back to the hallway – Mike looked at the map and analyzed it.

"Mike, point us in the right direction," I said.

"We go that way."

We followed Mike down the hall and came to an elevator. I pressed the call button on the wall. After a moment, it had arrived. The elevator was quite roomy inside. In addition, it had music playing. Looking at the console, it appeared we were on the lowest floor in Mantor's mansion – it may not seem much on the outside, but his place was quite vast underground. Laura went over to the console and pressed the button to go up. Once the doors closed, who knew what to expect on the other floors.

LABORATORY LUNACY
13

The elevator rose to the next floor – a computer voice announced the floor identification prior to opening the doors.

"Level A-1, Biomes."

Once the elevator doors opened, we saw a hall full of cubicles with various biomes in each. The area seemed to be "L" shaped. It went straight down and hooked left. We decided to explore the floor to see if we could find anything useful or an alternate exit.

"Wow, look at all these biome cells," said Sandra.

"This is quite interesting," said Chris.

"Man, there are a lot of them," said Laura.

"What the hell is he doing with these guys? He better not be experimenting on them," said Brooke.

Walking down the hall, we saw all sorts of humanoid creatures. Most cells had both genders of the species – some had only one gender. Biomes ranged from lush jungle-like environments to water filled aquariums.

We turned the corner and noticed a door thirty feet away.

"Marc, Chris, and I will check out this door and see if it leads us out of here," I said.

"While you guys do that, we'll secure the area," said Lucky.

Marc, Chris, and I went over to the door and opened it, revealing a small office with a couple of vertical file cabinets, a copy machine, and a desk.

"I wonder if there is any information we can find relating to those BIO-LM experiments," said Marc.

"Let's take a look around and see if we find anything," I said.

I looked around the desk and in the draws. Marc looked to see if he could find any secret doors or compartments. Chris looked through the vertical files and pulled out a manila folder.

"Guys, I found something," said Chris.

Chris put the folder on the desk and we looked at it. On the cover, it said "Top Secret" and on the tab, it said "Project BIO-LM."

"Looks like the bio-experiment Mantor's working on," said Marc.

I opened the folder and looked at the contents. Mantor built some kind of biomechanical creature that uses an advanced combat system – some kind of killing machine of some sort.

"It appears to be a combination of robotics and organic materials," said Marc.

"In other words a biomechanical super soldier," I added.

"I'm afraid to see what this thing looks like in person," said Chris.

"We need this info – It's too cumbersome to carry around a manila folder."

"Why don't we make copies using the copier?" asked Marc.

"Yeah, that will work," said Chris.

Marc pulled out all the important information and went over to the copier to make copies.

"Are you guys done yet?" asked Lucky while outside the door.

"We're finishing up – We're copying some information related to his experiments," I replied.

"What you should do is photocopy your ass and leave it on his desk with a big 'F-U' on it."

"Shall I do the honors?" asked Brooke.

After Marc made the copies, we put everything back in its place and left. While in the office, Bill recorded some footage of the biomes on his video camera – the more evidence, the better.

"Okay guys, let's get out of here – We gathered a fair amount of info," I said.

We went back to the elevator and got in. Mike looked at the floor plan of the mansion and located another elevator on the next floor. Hopefully, it would lead us out of here.

Laura pushed the button on the console and the elevator started to go up. Who knew what the next floor had.

"Is this the same song that was playing when we first got on this elevator?" asked Brooke.

"I believe it is," answered Talmar.

"Yeah, you're right – How boring, they only have one song?" said Jason.

"It would be better if they put on some old-school Hip-Hop – I'd be the most lit dog on this elevator, man," said Lucky.

The elevator reached the next floor and the computer voice spoke.

"Level A-2, Laboratory."

Something told me we'd meet Mantor's freakish creations here – all of us felt uneasy about what lied ahead.

The doors opened revealing a short white hall with a door at the end. We exited the elevator and proceeded to the door. A hand scanner terminal stood adjacent to it. Lucky opened the console, revealing the control board. He inserted his hacking cables and hacked away.

"Hand scanners, flawed as damn," said Lucky.

Within a minute, the door opened.

"Too easy," said Lucky.

"Sweet, dude," Roller added.

The door opened, revealing a laboratory full of tables and strange specimens. On the opposite side of the lab, the door to the other elevator can be seen.

"Okay, the elevator is just over there. Whatever you do, do not touch anything," I ordered.

We carefully walked our way through the lab. A section, near the elevator door, caught our eyes.

"What the hell is that?" asked Brooke.

"Oh... My..." said Sandra, covering her mouth in shock.

"God damn," said Lucky.

This strange specimen appeared to be a feminine torso suspended in a water tank with no arms, legs or even a head. It had tan reptilian skin and wires interweaved throughout the body. A contraption surrounded the pelvic area and a tube connected the piece to the bottom of the tank. It was eerily reminiscent of H.R. Geiger's artwork.

"This is the strangest thing I've ever seen, dude," said Roller.

"What the hell is that?" asked Rebekah.

"Eww," said Laura.

"What the frack..." said Charles.

"It seems it's a process for cloning," said Talmar.

"How's that? Wouldn't cloning be done in a petri dish?" asked Marc.

"That's how normal cloning is done. This is the dark side of science, my friends."

"What makes it so dark?" asked Brooke.

"This is an actual torso of a female individual," started Talmar, "As you can see, the normal features have been surgically removed. The wires connected to the lower abdomen are stimulating the ovaries causing them to release ova. This tube connected to the base of the contraption is collecting them."

"I think I'm going to be sick – That is legitimately disgusting," said Sandra, turning away in disgust.

"So, Mantor is using an actual dead woman's body to collect ovum?" I asked.

"Precisely," replied Talmar.

"Alrighty then... I think we've seen enough..." I said, turning to the exit door in disgust.

We walked away, went straight to the elevator, and got in. Seeing Mantor's specimen was quite disturbing. Why would he need a cloning process? Surely, he's not thinking of cloning himself – there must be another reason. Having a crazy contraption like that looks like he had an assembly line of some sort. Think about it, something to collect thousands of ova at a fast and efficient rate is an indication for a large process with multiple products. Could this be related to Project BIO-LM?

Laura pushed the button on the console and the elevator started to go up one extra floor. Unfortunately, it did not lead to the surface. Mike looked at the map and saw there were two more facilities until we reach the elevator leading up to the main floor. Our next stop, according to the map, was a two part warehouse. In the back of my mind, I had a feeling this warehouse stored more of Mantor's freakish creations. We prepared ourselves for the worst.

The elevator ride seemed a little longer than usual but after a couple of minutes, we had arrived at our destination. Once again, the computer voice spoke,

"Level B, Cryonics."

Before the elevator doors opened, I felt we would encounter something that will haunt our nightmares for a long time.

FREAKISH AND CREEPISH
14

After the doors opened, we went down a hallway with a door at the end. Fortunately, Lucky did not have to hack it. We opened the door and saw rows upon rows of cryogenically frozen creatures.

"This is insane," said Marc.

"There must be hundreds of them," said Evan.

"What the hell are these things?" asked Rebekah.

"This is what Mantor is using that female body for – He's cloning an army," I said.

"These must be the products of Project BIO-LM," said Chris.

"I'm going back," said Jason.

"You ain't going anywhere, J," said Evan.

We slowly walked into the facility. Approaching the tubes, I looked in to get a closer view of the specimen. It stood about six feet tall, had a fairly large build, and tan reptilian skin. These creatures appeared to be modified lizard men. It had a machine gun of some sort attached to its right arm. Looking up at the head, it had no eyes – just blank sockets with a possible image capturing device embedded in the skull. Mantor made some kind of cybernetic killing machine – I hoped we did not have to face such a monstrosity.

"Look at all the wires on these guys – Looks like some freakish and creepish creature Mantor is making," said Mike.

"Yeah, they're very creepy looking," said Laura.

"Let me record this on my camera," said Bill.

As we moved further into the warehouse, it started to feel like a maze. Nearing the end of the tube labyrinth, Laura notified us of something.

"Guys, this tube says 'Status: Malfunction' on top."

I looked at the other tubes. Normal looking ones said "Status: Normal" on top – others had the "Status: Malfunction." Not far from our position, we saw a security door up on a higher platform. In this section of the warehouse, the two parts were separated by this door – I ordered everyone to proceed to it immediately. Once again we had to get Lucky to crack the code. When I looked back at the cryo-tubes, I noticed a few others had the "Status: Malfunction" signs. Something did not seem right.

"Okay guys, it will probably take a couple of minutes," said Lucky.

"Get to it Luck, I see more with the bad warning above them," I said.

"Guys, one is moving over there," exclaimed Evan.

"Evan and Charles, defend this point," I ordered.

"Got it."

One of the creatures broke the glass tube and bashed its way out. Evan and Charles stood their ground and prepared for an attack. More creatures began breaking out of their cases. They walked slowly and heavily like a zombie.

"Should we fire?" asked Charles.

"Wait for it…"

The creatures approached. One lifted its machine gun and the barrels started to rotate. Luckily for us, it had no ammo. It looked at its gun and decided to go kamikaze. Then, all of them began running at us. Evan and Charles opened fire on the creatures. Bill, Mike, Laura, and Jason supplied extra firepower for them.

"Take 'em down," shouted Charles.

These creatures took plenty of punishment from the six. We needed extra power to fully incapacitate the onslaught – Brooke was the answer.

"Brooke, assault opposition," I ordered.

"With pleasure," he replied, cracking his knuckles.

Brooke went in to combat the creatures. Bullets softened them up making it easier to take them down using brute force. Sparks came out from the creatures' cybernetic connections as Brooke tore them to pieces. The onslaught had been stopped cold.

"Excellent work," I said.

"Okay guys, the door is unlocked," said Lucky.

We walked through and went down a short hallway with a security door at the end – it said "Warehouse Section A" on it.

"Hope Mantor doesn't mind the mess," said Brooke.

"It'll take him a long time to mop this up – In the end, we'll be mopping the floors with his dumb ass," said Lucky.

"Amen to that," I added.

After approaching the security door, Lucky began hacking the security console. God only knows what the next area is like.

WHERE IN THE WAREHOUSE ARE WE?
15

The door opened and in front of us was a massive warehouse.

"Man, this is some warehouse," said Bill.

"Mantor's mansion may not seem much on the outside but my God, there's a whole mess of stuff underground," said Marc.

"Looks like we're boxed in," said Jason.

"Heh, good one, dude," Roller added.

"Mike, are you able to lead us through this maze of boxes?" I asked.

"I'll see what I can do," he replied.

Mike took the lead and we followed him through the labyrinth of boxes. After a few twists and turns, Mike signaled us he had located the exit. A Minotaur guarded the area – it would be too risky to engage such a beast. We needed another plan…

"What are we going to do?" asked Rebekah.

"I could try and knock him out," suggested Brooke.

"Too risky, Brooke – He'd kill you in an instant," said Talmar.

"Maybe, I can talk with him," I said.

"I don't know, man," said Mike.

"Well, I'm stumped," said Brooke.

"There's got to be another way," said Chris.

Before calling it quits, Laura spoke up,

"I have an idea – Roller, I need you."

"Me, dude?"

"Yes, you... dude."

Laura picked up Roller and both went towards the Minotaur. We thought Laura and Roller were done for. Surely, a five-foot tall girl and a short canine humanoid would get creamed by this big guy.

"Laura, where are you going?" asked Rebekah.

"Laura, you'll get yourself killed," said Marc, frantically.

They approached the Minotaur – he stepped forward heavily. Laura stood her ground and held Roller tightly. The guard knelt down and spoke with a deep voice.

"What are you doing here little one?"

"My friends and I escaped Mantor because he's really mean – We just want to go home – Can we use the elevator... please?"

"I'm sorry but I can't let you do that – Besides, if he saw you here, he'd kill you. However, for a nice little human girl like yourself, I don't want him hurting you."

"Pretty please..."

Roller made a sad pooch face while Laura acted cute. The Minotaur seemed so touched by Laura's innocence and cuteness he eventually gave in.

"Very well – Tell your friends to come out."

We came out and proceeded over to Laura's position. The Minotaur appeared perplexed.

"Anthonian's helping humans? Explain."

"Let me put it to you this way – Your boss is a psycho," said Brooke.

"Mantor has secret experiments that are quite disturbing and unethical. In the second half of this warehouse, there is a cryogenics section with biomechanical specimens created using an illegal cloning process," explained Talmar.

"Here's some video footage I filmed on our way here," said Bill, showing the footage on his camera.

Marc also showed the Minotaur the copies of Mantor's secret and illegal experimentations we found in the biome section. The Minotaur, surprised and appalled, said,

"This is madness," he started, "I can't believe Mantor is doing such things. Let me come with you."

We got on the elevator and Laura hit the button on the console. The doors closed and the elevator started to ascend.

CONFRONTATION
16

We arrived on the main floor – the doors opened. The Minotaur exited first and checked if the coast was clear – he signaled us to follow him.

"Guys, stay low," I ordered.

We neared a corner and waited. The Minotaur gave us the okay to proceed. Walking into the lobby of the mansion, we heard a gunshot – our Minotaur friend froze and dropped to the ground making a big thump – we noticed he had been shot in the head. Near the entrance, there stood Mantor with a Desert Eagle pistol along with Sphinx wielding an Uzi.

"What a fool he is to be helping you," said Mantor.

"You son of a…" shouted Brooke.

"Go ahead, try and attack me. I can easily kill you like I did to him. Sphinx, help me keep them back."

"Yes, dear."

"It's over Mantor – We discovered what you've been doing and it's time to face justice," I said.

"How did you like my experiments?"

"Disgusting."

"We know everything, Mantor. You won't escape the law this time," said Sandra.

"Too bad you won't live to tell anyone."

Mantor prepared to fire at us – We retreated to the elevator for cover.

"If any of you follow, you will die."

Mantor and Sphinx left the lobby and escaped on an off-road golf cart. Laura ran over to the Minotaur and broke down in tears. Marc went over to comfort her.

"I'm sorry, Laura, he's gone."

"Mantor must be stopped," exclaimed Sandra.

"His ass is mine," said Brooke.

"Guys, I think it's time we slam Mantor with the hand of justice. Let's go out there and get him," I ordered.

"Gonna pimp smack his ass," said Lucky.

We regrouped and exited through the lobby doors. Tire tracks can be seen on the ground leading into some nearby vegetation.

"Looks like he went that way," I said.

"He went in there?" asked Lucky.

"I'll navigate through it – I've done this before," said Talmar.

"We'll cover you," said Marc.

"Talmar – You head in first," I ordered.

"Got it."

"Evan and Charles, cover him up front."

"Roger."

"Chris, Bill, and Mike – Cover behind them."

"Got it."

"Marc and I will stand behind those three – Rebekah, Laura, and Jason – Stand behind me and Marc."

"Got it."

"Lucky and Roller, stay near me and Marc."

"Roger."

"Sandra and Brooke, cover the sides up front with Evan and Charles."

"Got it."

"Let's move."

We followed Talmar into the vegetation. Mantor must have millions of dollars to have all this property. Why does it always seem money falls into the wrong hands? To be honest, I don't know any villain who is poor. Anyway, we moved further into the vegetation and then Talmar picked up Mantor's trail.

"I'm picking up a scent and I believe it is gasoline from Mantor's cart. I believe he went that direction," said Talmar.

Further in, the jungle became darker – the dense vegetation blocked out the sunlight.

"Why is it so dark?" asked Charles.

"The more trees, the more shade," replied Talmar.

"Does that include fog? I noticed further down it seems to be foggy," said Evan.

"Ah, yes, it seems to be very humid in this part."

After a few minutes, Sandra came over to me.

"Hey, Sandra, what's up?" I asked.

"I'm a little uneasy about this part of the jungle. I was wondering if I could stand by you for a little," she replied.

"I see why not."

I figured it wouldn't hurt for Sandra to stay close to me. Talmar had a good amount of cover up front.

Moving further into the jungle, we started hearing activity up in the trees. We paused and looked around. Further down the path, I noticed a figure and then it vanished. I couldn't tell what it was but I knew we were not alone.

"This place gives me the creeps, dude," said Roller.

"I heard something coming in that direction," said Charles.

"Be on your guard everyone," I ordered.

Continuing onward, we came across a marsh with shallow water.

"Something doesn't seem right. I could've have sworn his scent was coming from this direction," said Talmar.

"Something tells me Mantor threw us off track somehow," said Brooke.

"Maybe he did come this way but probably junked the cart and then walked through," said Lucky.

"Hey dudes, look over there – I think I see a bit of the cart sticking out of the water," said Roller.

"Though it appears he's right," said Talmar.

"I guess we proceed through the water then," I said.

Before any of us could head through the marsh, more sounds of movement can be heard. Sandra moved closer to me in a protective way. She looked up at the trees and then checked the surroundings.

"I sense something, Alan – Stay close."

"Roger – Standing by."

Sandra sensed something that didn't bode well with her. After a moment, we went into the marsh. Rebekah and Laura were quite displeased they had to walk through dirty water in their high priced shoes they bought at the mall. It was no problem for Sandra, Brooke, Talmar, Lucky, and Roller since they're already barefoot.

The water felt cool and looked very muddy. Its depth appeared to be between the ankle and the knee. As we got further, the water became a little deeper – nearly waist deep. Lucky and Roller had difficulty in this section – Evan and Charles volunteered to carry them on their backs.

Evan carried Lucky and Charles carried Roller.

"Eww, mud is getting into my shoes," said Rebekah.

"You think that's bad, my pants are wet," said Jason.

"They were probably wet before you got in the water, J," said Evan.

"Very funny…"

"My doggie senses are tingling – We ain't alone in this water, man," said Lucky, sniffing the air.

Within a blink of an eye, a creature from under the water popped up in front of Rebekah. She let out a big scream as the creature grabbed her and dragged her underwater.

"Beka," shouted Laura.

"What the hell was that thing?" exclaimed Marc.

"It's going that way," shouted Evan.

The creature had a humanoid upper torso and a serpent-like lower half. After a few seconds, Rebekah came up, wrestling the swamp monster.

"Shoot the damn thing," shouted Rebekah.

Laura whipped out her MP5K and shot the creature down. Rebekah had a couple of scratches but nothing major.

"Rebekah, are you okay?" I asked.

"Barely – That ass messed up my hair, got me all soaked, and I broke a couple of my nails."

"Calm down sweet cheeks – Be thankful you're alive," said Brooke.

Rebekah gave Brooke a dirty look.

"Nice shootin', Laura," I said.

"Thanks."

We made it to the other side of the marsh and continued. About a hundred feet away, there appeared to be a clearing. While walking in the direction of it, something from the shrubbery darted out and tackled me to the ground. To my surprise, it was a crocodile man.

"Ah – Get off," I shouted.

"Alan," shouted Sandra.

"Hang in there," shouted Brooke.

Sandra and Brooke got the croc-man off before he could take a bite out of me. Brooke grabbed the croc-man and threw him against a tree, knocking him out. Sandra helped me up.

"Are you okay?" asked Sandra.

"Yeah, I'm okay. Just a little startled but I'm fine."

"What the hell was that thing?" asked Charles.

"That was a crocodile man. They're just like regular lizard men but a lot more aggressive. Once they catch their prey, they can tear them to shreds quickly," said Brooke.

"I hate those guys, they're so primitive and disgusting," said Sandra.

Soon after, more croc-men started to emerge from their hiding spots.

"Dudes, we got company," said Roller.

"Damn, we're surrounded," said Lucky.

"What do we do?" asked Laura.

"Stand your ground," I ordered.

The croc-men began getting closer and closer. Then one of them suddenly dropped down next to Jason, ready to attack him. Rebekah quickly fired at the croc-man, saving Jason. After the first shot, the croc-men charged at us. Evan and Charles took down enemies from one direction while Chris, Bill, and Mike took down more from another. Lucky and Roller fired at some in the trees. Brooke threw a few croc-men around and whacked them hard in the face. I took down some opposition from all over.

"I need some help here," shouted Rebekah.

I noticed Lucky just finishing off his wave of enemies – I called out to him.

"Lucky, Beka needs cover fire," I ordered.

"I'm on it," he replied.

While Lucky went to assist Rebekah, Sandra seemed to be in a jam herself. A croc-man grabbed her wrists and looked as if he was trying to bite her. I went in and unloaded a couple of shells on the fiend. Sandra lost her footing and fell to the ground – I went to help her up.

"Are you okay, Sandra?"

Sandra nodded and smiled at me – her eyes followed me with precision.

"Thank you."

"Got your back, Sandra – Now let's return to kicking some croc-man butt."

"You got it," she said, smiling.

I glanced back and saw her beat down two croc-men. She round house kicked the first then flipped the other one over her back. I sure was impressed with her combat abilities. Since she had everything under control, I noticed Marc becoming overwhelmed by a few hostiles. I ran over to his position and fired my gun, taking down some of the enemies surrounding him. Marc took down the final two. Soon after, four croc-men started charging towards us.

"Al, we got company."

"Alan, Marc, get down," shouted Charles.

Marc and I ducked down as Charles ran towards us. He then jumped off of our backs towards the oncoming croc-men, firing his pistols. He successfully took two down with ease. Marc and I mopped up the other two.

"Hiyaaa – Yeah, take that scaly," exclaimed Charles, spin-kicking a croc-man in the face.

We finished off the wave of croc-men and the rest retreated back into the vegetation.

"They're retreating – Onslaught ceasing," Mike called out.

"Finally – I thought that would never end," said Brooke.

"Is everyone alright?" I asked.

"Yeah, a little bruised but okay," Evan answered.

"Let's move out," I ordered.

We approached the clearing. To our surprise, it looked like we made it to the other side of the island, near the shoreline about a hundred yards away. The clearing consisted of a large dirt field with three abandoned buildings adjacent to a hill to our left. Directly in front of us were a few towers of cages containing human hostages. To the right of those were a few clusters of crates. It appeared to be too easy to get to the cages. I had a feeling Mantor waited for us somewhere in the area. It's time for a showdown!

SHOWDOWN
17

We walked out into the clearing and looked all around – no sign of Mantor or Sphinx. Taking advantage of the situation, we went over to the cages to see how to free the hostages.

"Oh, my God – There's a lot a people in these," said Marc.

The people began yelling and calling out for help. I don't think they knew that if they didn't pipe down, they'd give away our position.

"Everyone, keep your voices down – We'll find a way – Just be patient," I ordered.

"Dammit, are these people stupid?" asked Chris.

"They'll blow our cover," Mike added.

"Let's find a way to open these cages. I noticed electrodes on the ground connected to them – There must be some kind of remote access," I said.

Power boxes were connected to the base of the cages. I asked Lucky if there was a way to override the locks.

"Lucky, can these be hacked into?" I asked.

He looked at it for a moment and noticed a problem.

"Damn – Mantor has this fail-safe mechanism in place. This would prevent us from tampering with it. We need to find a switch of some sort to deactivate the locks on the cages."

While we looked all around the cages, Laura signaled us to come over to her. She showed us a small cliffhanger – the slope looked like it went at least thirty-three degrees downward. At the base of the hill, cages and cargo boxes sat near the shoreline. In addition, a helipad with two Black Hawk helicopters was on standby.

Before we could do anything, we heard an engine roar from within some vegetation nearby. We looked back and saw a military issue Hummer speed out. In the driver seat was Sphinx and she looked pissed. A set of guns deployed on the roof of the vehicle and started firing plasma bolts at us.

"Incoming," shouted Evan.

"Duck and Cover," exclaimed Charles.

"Everyone, to the buildings," I ordered.

We scrambled to the three busted down buildings. I ran into the first one with Marc, Evan, Charles, Sandra, and Brooke, taking cover until we had the opportunity to fire back. If any of us got hit with plasma, it would be fatal.

In the last building, we could hear our friends firing at Sphinx's vehicle. Since she was distracted, I ordered Evan and Charles to open fire on her.

"Evan and Charles, open fire on Sphinx," I ordered.

"What if she fires back at us?" asked Evan.

"Once the plasma turret turns in our direction, cease fire and go for cover."

"Let's do this," said Charles.

The two fired at the vehicle. Fluids began leaking from the Hummer. Sphinx discontinued firing at the last building and turned in our direction. Evan and Charles went for cover. The group in the second building began firing at Sphinx. After a moment, the turret started to go on fire and became disabled. The vehicle went up in smoke and had been incapacitated.

"Vehicle down," shouted Marc.

Sphinx got out and I gave the order for everyone to go after her. She drew her Uzi but Jason shot it out of her hands from a distance with a pistol.

"Hold it right there," I shouted, pointing my shotgun at Sphinx.

"Go ahead, kill me, human."

"We're not, but sure enough, we're going put you behind bars for obstruction of justice."

"Brooke, hold her," ordered Marc.

Brooke grabbed Sphinx and held her arms behind her back tightly. She struggled a bit but he made sure she remained still.

"You are in violation of justice – Tell us where Mantor is," I exclaimed.

"Why should I tell you?" asked Sphinx, in a snobbish way.

"Answer the question, Sphinx," ordered Sandra.

"Aren't you Mister Shaanti's daughter?"

"Who wants to know?"

"Answer the question or I'll break your wrists," ordered Brooke.

"You'll die before you get to find out."

"Do we have to ask you another three times?" I asked.

"Maybe."

"She ain't speaking," said Chris.

"I have an idea. Can I borrow your shotgun Rebekah?" asked Charles.

She gave him the shotgun. He then pointed it at Sphinx point blank at her chest.

"Okay, Sphinx, how would you like a big hole blasted into you?"

"You wouldn't dare."

"Yes, I would. If you tell us where Mantor is, you'll leave with no bodily injury. You'll be nice, safe... and firm... and round..." said Charles, staring at Sphinx's breasts.

"Charles..." I said, trying to get him back on track.

"Sorry – So, what'll it be, Sphinx?" Charles finished.

"Take a look near the vegetation. He's over there in that mech-suit."

We looked towards the vegetation and saw Mantor walking out with this big mech-warrior, thumping its way over. Sphinx elbowed Brooke in the gut and got loose. She ran off and hid somewhere in nearby shrubbery.

"Holy crap," said Brooke.

"Dear God," said Talmar.

"That is one big friggin' mech," said Evan.

"I think we should run," said Charles.

"Not a bad idea, Charles. Everyone, fall back to the buildings," I ordered.

"Well, the little team of heroes have made it this far – I'm impressed. Now let's see if you can dodge armor piercing bullets from two mounted miniguns as well as rockets from my rocket launcher. If you do survive that, I'll let you have some plasma to eat with my mounted plasma cannon. Who do you think's going to win? I know you all won't." said Mantor, through a loudspeaker on the mech.

Mantor started to open fire. The miniguns tore through the walls of the buildings – we had to find better cover. Evan, Marc, and I ran over to the crates near the cages. Our current weapons were useless against the mech. Machineguns barely made dents and shotgun blasts ricocheted off the armor. The only way we could beat such a tank is with better guns. Thankfully, our answer was next to us.

"Man, what are we gonna do?" asked Evan

"Our weapons are useless against that thing," said Marc.

"Guys, these crates may have something to help us," I said.

The crate next to us had the word "Weapons" on it. A crowbar sat adjacent to it on the ground.

"Evan, see if you can open this crate with that crowbar," I ordered.

"I'll try – Eat your heart out, Freeman."

Evan started to pry open the sides and eventually got it open.

"Okay boys, dig in," said Evan.

"Wow, look at these weapons," said Marc.

Inside were four weapons with some ammunition. First weapon: an automatic loading rocket launcher called the RL-16. Each mag contained eight mini-rockets and loaded from the bottom of the gun. Second weapon: two smaller, rifle-sized, weapons called the PR-500. They fired plasma bolts and ran on energy cells. Last weapon: the Battery Force Gun – a large, single-shot, warhead launcher.

Marc grabbed the PR-500 and Evan grabbed the RL-16. Both took extra ammo just in case. I took the B-F-G. Something told me it would be powerful enough to destroy Mantor's mech. It sounded *unreal* but I had one shot – I had to make it count.

"Guys, I only have one shot with this gun. Try and weaken him – Disable his guns so I have a clear shot at him," I said.

"Roger that," said Evan.

"Let's do this," said Marc.

"Let's tag 'em and bag 'em," I said.

Marc and Evan came around the crate and began firing at Mantor's mech. We could already see the plasma and rockets damaging it pretty well.

"Hit 'em hard," shouted Marc.

Marc disabled the mounted rocket launcher on the mech. At least it bought our buddies some time to scramble. Evan fired a couple of rockets at the mounted miniguns and blew them right off. Mantor turned in our direction and only had one weapon left… the plasma cannon.

"The plasma cannon is still active," shouted Marc.

"Someone shoot the damn plasma cannon," I ordered.

Bill took a hand grenade and threw it at the cannon. The grenade got stuck in a little tight spot where the cannon met the mech body. It exploded and disabled the gun.

"Nice shot, Bill – Okay guys, lure him near the hill leading down," I ordered

"Affirmative," said Marc.

I got ready to fire the warhead at Mantor. Marc and Evan weakened the mech's armor a little more. Mantor neared the edge of the cliffhanger – if this warhead had enough force, it would knock him over.

"Clear," shouted Evan.

"Fire in the hole," shouted Marc.

"Dodge this," I shouted.

I fired the gun and the recoil blew me back a bit. Marc and Evan cleared the area before impact. Within a matter of seconds, the warhead struck the mech causing a large explosion, blowing Mantor straight over the cliffhanger. A few pieces of the mech remained and all we heard was twisted metal rolling down the hill.

Afterwards, everybody came over to me. We walked over to the hill and clambered down to investigate the wreckage below.

"Hey guys, I videotaped Mantor getting blown over the edge. It looks friggin' amazing. I may actually put that in a video and turn it into an action movie trailer," said Bill.

"How awesome would that be…" said Mike.

"It would be so awesome that your head will explode into candy."

We got down to where Mantor's mech landed. Some thought he was defeated but others, including myself, had a feeling he was still alive.

"With a blow like that, he couldn't have survived," said Chris.

"Mantor is tricky. I wouldn't be too surprised if he made it out alive," said Sandra.

Within the dust and smoke, we saw a figure standing.

"Uh... guys? He's still alive," said Charles.

Mantor stood in front of us, enraged and poised to kill. He wasn't going to go down until he killed all of us.

"I'm not finished yet – You think you can beat me? Well let's see how you handle my next weapon," shouted Mantor.

Mantor pulled out a large gun from his mech. It appeared to be a grenade launcher of some sort.

"Prepare to meet your doom," he shouted.

Mantor would not rest until we were exterminated. It was now time to have the ultimate face off with the ultimate villain.

THE ULTIMATE CHALLENGE
18

Mantor began firing his weapon forcing us to find cover. A grenade flew past me and blew up a crate full of guns. The weapons survived the explosion. I went over to grab a PR-500 and took cover behind the cages.

Explosions echoed throughout the area. I took a glance and saw a few of my buddies hurt badly. Talmar, Chris, and Mike dragged some of the injured behind a row of cages. I darted over there to give them cover fire.

"Guys, take the injured further down the row of cages – they'll be better hidden," I ordered.

"Roger," replied Chris and Mike.

Laura, Bill, Jason, and Rebekah were among the injured. Fortunately, they didn't suffer major wounds. At most, some had bad cuts on their arms or legs. After helping Chris and Mike, I told them to defend everyone.

"Come on – Give me your best shot," shouted Mantor.

I neared the corner of the cages and prepared to dash over to the rest of my friends. They were located behind a set of crates across the way.

"Where are you Alan?" shouted Mantor, "Show yourself."

I readied the PR-500, took a deep breath, and ran.

"There you are," shouted Mantor.

I heard the popping sound of a grenade being launched and dove behind the nearest crate. The grenade blew up a couple of boxes nearby. It was a close one...

"Alan," shouted Sandra.

"I'm okay – Hold your positions," I shouted.

Mantor fired one more shot near my position. I dashed out of the area before impact. Fortunately, the explosion didn't get me and Mantor ran out of ammo. I came around the crate and fired the plasma gun. He evaded my firepower and hid behind a crate closest to the cages. As Mantor ran, he picked up a Chaingun on the ground near the crate he destroyed earlier. I ran over to Marc, Sandra, Evan, and Charles. Lucky and Roller stood by a smaller crate fifteen feet away from our position.

"Guys, he's got a Chaingun," I said.

"That's not good," said Marc.

"What do we do?" asked Charles.

"We need Brooke," said Sandra.

"Does anyone know where he is?" I asked.

We heard a roar and looked in the direction from whence it came. Brooke stood atop the cages and then dropped down on Mantor. He smacked the Chaingun out of Mantor's hands and went straight into hand-to-hand combat.

"You're going down, Mantor," exclaimed Brooke.

"Give me your best shot, Mister Stone."

Brooke threw a few good punches and nailed him in the face. Mantor used more scratch attacks and we could see the damages on Brooke.

"I'm gonna kick your ass for what you've done to Sandra," started Brooke, "You deserve every ounce of pain I put into you."

As Brooke was about to strike him with a powerful blow, Mantor threw dirt at Brooke's face, blinding him. Mantor, now being able to attack back, started punching Brooke in the stomach and across the face. Charles immediately ran out and charged towards the action. He grabbed Mantor from behind and got him into a half nelson. This bought Brooke enough time to get back up.

"Forget knocking," exclaimed Charles.

"Get off you damn mammal," exclaimed Mantor.

Mantor flipped Charles over his shoulder and slammed him into the ground. Charles got up and attacked Mantor aggressively.

"You're going down snake man," exclaimed Charles.

He got a few hits off him, however, it wasn't effective enough. Mantor round house kicked Charles and then went to grab the Chaingun. Brooke came at Mantor but wound up getting knocked out as well. We needed to get those guys over to Talmar ASAP.

"Sandra and Evan, get Charles and Brooke over to Talmar – We'll cover you," I ordered.

"Got it," acknowledged Evan.

"Will you be okay?" asked Sandra.

"We'll be fine – We'll hold him off as long as we can. Now get going before he sees you as the primary target," I replied.

Sandra and Evan ran off to help Charles and Brooke. As Mantor was about to look in their direction, Lucky and Roller opened fire to divert his attention. Sandra and Evan made it over to Brooke and Charles and moved them over to Talmar.

"Play time is over," exclaimed Mantor.

Mantor started to fire at us. The crates took heavy damage causing us to seek better cover.

"Man, he's *really* pissed off," said Lucky.

Evan came out from behind the cages and started to run across back over to us. While doing so, he fired a couple of rockets from the RL-16. Mantor ran for cover before the rockets hit the ground near him. Evan came over to us to give a status report.

"Sandra is going to hold a spot near Talmar for a moment. I'm also low on rockets, man. I'll use the C2AR instead," said Evan.

"So, what's the plan?" asked Marc.

"We need to get him on multiple angles," I started to say, "Evan, take a position at the corner of the cages," I ordered.

I pointed to the spot where I wanted Evan to standby. He nodded in acknowledgment.

"Lucky and Roller, take position behind the crates to our left. Pick him off the best you can."

"Roger that."

"Marc, take him from the side of the crate bundle on the right."

"Got it."

"Let's move out."

I looked at the ammo gauge on the plasma gun and I had very little charge left. I decided to use up whatever I had left and take down Mantor with the shotgun.

"I've knocked out most of your comrades. How about you surrender?" said Mantor.

Evan began firing the C2AR from his position. Mantor dove out of the way. The C2AR jammed – Mantor took advantage and attacked him. He knocked the gun out of his hands and threw a punch. Evan dodged the strike.

"Alright green boy, you want to play rough? Let's go."

Evan threw a few punches. He attacked low and got Mantor in the stomach. Mantor came around and got Evan in an uppercut. He got back up and went all out. Mantor scratched Evan across the chest a couple of times and then kneed him in the stomach. Then he finished him with one final right hook to the face.

"Not bad, human. Still, you are too easy," said Mantor.

"Bitch," said Evan, getting the last word out.

After Evan fell to Mantor, Lucky and Roller came out firing their Uzis. Mantor quickly drew his Desert Eagle and shot both Uzis out of their paws. He quickly caught up to them, grabbed Roller, and threw him at a large box, knocking him out cold. Lucky was pissed.

"Alright, man whore, no one does that to my brutha and gets away with it."

"Heh... Bring it on, mutt."

Mantor threw a punch. Lucky dodged the shot and returned with a counter attack. He gave a powerful right hook followed by a powerful left hook. Lucky then did a summersault kick, throwing him off guard. Mantor then grabbed him and threw him at a large box. I could tell Luck was injured.

"Good boy, stay," said Mantor, taunting at Lucky.

"This isn't over, man whore," Lucky replied, in pain.

Afterwards, Marc came around his hiding spot and started to fire plasma. Mantor went for cover and snuck a shot at him. The bullet hit Marc in his right leg – I heard him yell in agony.

"Come out Alan – I want a worthy opponent, not your worthless friends," exclaimed Mantor.

While Mantor tried to find me, I snuck around some boxes and dashed over to Marc's position.

"Alan, take my plasma gun – You got to finish him off."

"I will shortly, but let me get you over to Talmar."

"Don't worry about me – Take Mantor down before he kills all of us."

"Marc, I'm getting you over to Talmar, now – Your leg is bleeding badly – The bullet literally went through your leg."

"Dammit."

Suddenly, Mantor came behind me. I turned slowly towards him. He pointed his Desert Eagle straight at my head.

"Remember what I said, Alan. You can't save everyone – Not even your friend here."

I thought it was going to be my last moment. Shot at point blank and being slain by the villain. Before I lost all hope, Sandra came behind Mantor and got him in a half nelson. She, too, pulled his arm and pointed the gun away from me.

"Alan, get Marc over to Talmar – I'll hold him off," Sandra ordered.

I helped Marc up and walked him over to Talmar. After helping him sit down, I gave Chris and Mike our plasma guns.

"Talmar, his leg is bleeding badly."

"Don't worry, I'll tend to him. Alan, go help Sandra. I feel she may have trouble taking on Mantor by herself."

"I'm on it."

I quickly ran back to check on Sandra – she was giving him hell.

"You'll pay for what you did to my parents," exclaimed Sandra.

Sandra threw a few good hooks right at him. Mantor began to attack back using his claws. I wanted to help Sandra but I did not have the right gun for the situation. If I fired my shotgun, not only would I hit Mantor, Sandra, too, would get hit. I had to wait for the right moment.

While this went on, I kept a careful eye on the situation. Sandra managed to pin Mantor to the ground.

"Time to finish you off," said Sandra.

Before Sandra could punch Mantor hard across the face, he grabbed her neck and threw her off of him. As she got back up, Mantor scratched her across the face and kicked her to the ground. Now, I had my opportunity. I came around the crate and opened fire. The blast knocked Mantor to the ground – he cried out in pain. I quickly went over to Sandra and helped her up.

"Hang on Sandra – I'm here," I said.

Sandra held her face, blood dripping over her hand. We made it over to Talmar and I could see my buddies looking nervous – I could tell by looking at their faces.

"Alan, since you're the only one left who is not incapacitated, you're our last hope to beat him," started Talmar, "I surely don't have the strength to face him and I need Chris and Mike to defend this position – It's up to you."

Sandra put her hand on my shoulder. We looked at each other for a moment and then she gave me a hug for good luck.

"You can do it, Alan – Just believe in yourself," she whispered in my ear.

I nodded to her and everyone else. I went back on the battlefield and looked at Mantor getting up. He shouted in rage, then looking at me with intent to kill. I walked out there and prepared myself.

"I am going to enjoy killing you," he said.

I remained silent – I just stared at him and remained focused.

"I suggest you surrender. You have no chance of beating me."

"I beg to differ, Mantor. Before we get down to the clichéd epic fight scene between hero and villain, let me ask you a question – Why do you hate humans so much?"

"You want to know? I'll tell you, boy," started Mantor, "It all started when I was a child, in the rainforest, with my parents. I played with my father and my mother just watched, sitting under a tree. Next thing I knew, there was a gunshot. I looked over to my mother and noticed she was hit. My father told me to run but I went over to my mother first. She told me to run as well, then she passed out – I knew she couldn't be saved. My father then again told me to run. I heard another gunshot when I made it to the clearing."

Mantor paused for a second. I could see the pain and agony in his eyes. He then continued.

"There, I was approached by a human poacher. He said, 'Well looky here, a little lizard boy. His skin would do well on the market.' Then I noticed another human coming out of the jungle with layers of Najanian flesh. They were using Najanian skin for currency. I managed to escape them and find a safe haven. I said to myself, 'One day, I'll make those humans suffer – I will have my revenge.' That is why I hate humans so much."

"Well, your story was very touching," I started to say, "Still not all humans are bad."

Pausing for a second, I then asked the other question – the one about Sandra's parents.

"The question still boggling my mind is, why did you kill Sandra's parents?"

"I had good reason..."

"I thought you were *for* your kind," I started to say, "Why did you kill your own kind?"

"I don't want to hear any more of this..."

"Was it worth all the rage you had towards the human race to go and kill another child's parents?"

"Shut up..."

"To make that child suffer the same fate you did? Do you think that was fair? Do you think it was fair for her to suffer like you did?"

"Enough of this..."

"Answer me, God dammit," I exclaimed.

"Her parents were a threat to me – They had to be liquidated," he replied with anger.

"Why must they feel the pain that you had, huh?" I started, "Same thing with the human race. Why should every single human suffer *your* pain?"

"Silence."

"What did some of these poor people do to you, huh? Did *they* kill your parents? No – It was only those damn poachers," I shouted.

"Enough," he shouted.

Everything went silent for a moment. Mantor stared at me with raging eyes.

"Mantor, look at yourself, look at what you are doing. Look at the people who you've hurt. Look at the crimes you've committed. Is sinning ever going to solve anything? You've murdered, you've destroyed, you've hated, you've harmed – Have any of those ever brought your parents back? Has any of that made your life any better?"

He stood there in silence.

"I lost my father a year ago and I'm not going out and killing people. Sure, it's traumatic when you lose a parent or even both. But you have to leave everything in the past and concentrate on the present. I still remember what happened the day when I found my father on the floor dying. I remember it so well, it haunts my nightmares. Am I letting that keep me back? No – I'm concentrating on what's going on right now."

I paused for a moment to catch a breath.

"Look at what you did to Sandra's parents. You did what those poachers did. You've slain them in cold blood. You made her feel the same pain that you felt when your parents were killed. Was it really necessary?"

Mantor looked away for a moment then back at me.

"You bring up a good point, boy. You are right," he started to say, "But, it is too late for me to change. I've done what I've done, and I need to finish what I have begun."

I started to get nervous – Mantor calmed down too easily – I readied my shotgun.

"You see, my whole life was a metaphorical version of Hell. Despite I had money, a wife that made love to me weekly, a successful business, and even the power to work with extraterrestrials and Hell itself, I was still not satisfied with my life," he started to say, "I wanted to die knowing I got my revenge."

I followed a bit of what he said – In short, he had gone insane. Mantor put down his Desert Eagle and readied his fists.

"Put down your weapon. Let's settle this like men."

I tossed the shotgun to the side and prepared for hand-to-hand combat. We approached each other and prepared to fight.

Mantor came at me with a few attacks but I stepped out of the way. He attempted to trip me but I jumped up in time and kicked him in the chest. Sadly, it didn't do much. The next attack was a right straight punch targeted at my stomach. I blocked his attack and grabbed his arm – I then pulled him and nailed him in the face with my elbow. Pushing him away, I kept my distance.

He lunged towards me, tackling me to the ground then revealing his fangs and hissing. It appeared he had a venomous bite just like a snake – small drops of venom dripped down his canines. I pushed him back with my knee and got up. He came back and scratched me across my chest. I then punched him in the face a couple of times with my right fist while holding him back with my left.

After pushing him away, he quickly came and scratched me a couple of times. Things began to go downhill. Mantor began coming at me with rage, beating me down to a pulp. He punched me across the face, got me a few times in the stomach, and got me a couple of times in the side of the ribs. I fell to the ground and got back up in agony. As I turned to face him, he kicked me in the gut, knocking me to the ground.

"Had enough, Alan?" asked Mantor, "Huh?" he said, kicking me hard from the side.

I painfully got up and faced him. He then came at me and grabbed my neck. He pinned me against the cages and looked at me with anger, then ripping off my armor and shirt. Mantor held the Guardian Emblem around my neck and looked at it for a moment.

"It's funny how The Guardians chose a human to be their champion. I'm so going to enjoy killing you."

Mantor pulled the emblem off my neck and tossed it aside. He then threw me to the ground behind him.

"You are weak – I think your friends pity you more than they like you. Have you ever thought of that? They couldn't give a damn if you died. You are nothing to them – A nobody."

As I got up, he started slashing me with his claws. Droplets of blood covered the ground. The last scratch from Mantor was across my face. I fell to the ground and Mantor stood there laughing at me.

"Why don't you just give up? Do you really think you have any chance?"

I got up with the remaining strength I had and started to charge at him. I yelled in rage and when I was about to punch him, he stepped out of the way, grabbed me, and wrapped his arm tightly around my neck, constricting me with a half-nelson.

"Look at you all mad – Let that anger fester – Let it consume you…"

"No – I will not."

"Do you think being good will ever get you anywhere?"

"Yes – It has – You see those people over there? Those are my friends – I earned them. The question I have for you, Mantor, where are your friends? Huh? Where's your wife? Huh? She couldn't give a crap about you. My friends care about me. What *you* say is a lie. Being good is what got me those friends – It got me love and respect – I may be a nobody to you, Mantor, but to them, I'm somebody special."

Within an instant, Sandra came from behind Mantor and got him off me.

"Get off of him, you monster," shouted Sandra.

Sandra dragged Mantor to the ground. He elbowed her in the gut and broke free. Mantor then slashed her across her shoulder. I took advantage of Sandra's distraction and attacked Mantor from behind. Unfortunately, he turned around too soon and threw a punch. I ducked down in time and came back up with an uppercut. Sandra grabbed Mantor around his neck and threw him to the ground. He retaliated by tripping her.

Mantor got back up and came at me quickly. He swung around me, wrapped his arm around my neck and then locked his jaws around my neck and shoulder region. The pain was unfathomable – I felt the venom dripping into my bloodstream. I let out a loud cry of anguish.

"No," Sandra shouted.

Sandra watched in disbelief. She couldn't believe what had just happened. Her shocked expression said it all. Mantor released me and pushed me towards her. I fell to the ground holding the area where Mantor bit me. Blood dripped over my hand and onto the ground. The venom began draining the life out of me – I felt feverish, my eyes became blurry, and my hearing a bit muffled. This must be what death felt like. Sandra came over to me immediately.

"Alan – No, no, no, no – Please no," said Sandra, choking up.

"Now you get to see another loved one die, Sandra. Maybe the best way for me to kill you is to break your heart."

Mantor laughed maniacally, then, out of nowhere, Brooke ambushes Mantor and knocks him down hard. Lucky, too, joined the party.

"How about I break your face, douche bag," said Brooke.

"I should snap those wings of yours."

"Yeah? And I should snap your neck – Let's go, asshole."

Brooke came at him with a rapid succession of punches and tail-whips. He then threw a powerful right hook and a powerful left hook. Lastly, he grabbed Mantor by the neck, lifted him up, and slammed him into the ground hard. Talk about an ultra-combo attack. Mantor had finally been K.O.'d. Lucky went over to him to get the final word out.

"You just got smoked, bitch."

Talmar ran over to us quickly.

"Talmar, Mantor poisoned him. Do you have an anti-toxin?" asked Brooke.

"I do – It won't hold him for long, though – We need to get him to a hospital immediately."

"Alan, stay with me – Stay with me – I don't want to lose you – Please don't die – Please," cried Sandra.

"Al, hang in there," said Lucky.

"We need transportation now," exclaimed Brooke.

Talmar injected the anti-toxin into my left arm. The venom had done a lot of damage and I was fading fast. I felt very weak and after a moment, I went unconscious. Queue third person mode! Whoosh!

* * * * * * *

After Alan blacked out, Lucky ran back over to everyone.

"Guys, we need to get Alan on the chopper – We gotta airlift him to the hospital pronto."

"Luck, what's going on?" asked Chris.

"Mantor poisoned him. Al's in bad shape, man – Let's get to those two choppers. Bro, you feelin' okay? Good, I need you to fly the other one, man."

"You can fly them?" asked Mike.

"Yeah, we can. Since we lived in an airport, obviously we learned how to fly aircrafts."

"Especially helicopters, dude."

"Let's move – Secure the choppers," Mike ordered.

"Get to the choppers," exclaimed Charles.

They ran over to the helicopters. Sandra carried Alan into the first one.

"Okay, I will operate chopper one. Bro, you take chopper two," said Lucky.

Sandra, Brooke, Talmar, Marc, Charles, and Evan went on the first helicopter. Chris, Bill, Mike, Rebekah, Laura, and Jason went on the other helicopter. Lucky and Roller started the choppers and lifted off.

"Yo, Talmar, guide me to the nearest hospital," ordered Lucky.

"Head northwest – You see that tall building over there with a helipad? That's where you go."

"Bro, follow me. There's room for only one chopper on the roof of the hospital. Locate another area to drop the team – You copy?"

"Roger that, Luck. I'll seek out another helipad in the vicinity, dude."

Lucky reached the top of the building and radioed the hospital regarding an emergency landing.

"Chopper one to hospital, do you read me?" radioed Lucky.

"Chopper one, this is Anthronia Hospital, do you copy…" replied a voice on the radio.

"I request permission to land on the helipad on the roof. We have an emergency situation. Occupant on chopper is in critical condition and requires immediate medical attention."

"Chopper One, you are clear to land. Security and medical personnel will be standing by."

"Roger, over and out."

Lucky proceeded to land the chopper on the roof. After a successful landing, medical personnel came out with a stretcher and made their way over.

"We need to get him inside immediately," ordered Talmar.

"Right away, Dr. Monitor," acknowledged a member of the emergency team.

"I'll catch up to you guys in a sec – Just go," said Lucky.

The team on the roof went through the rooftop doors and down in an elevator. Lucky radioed his brother.

"Bro, Alan's inside and I'll be catching up to the rest. What's your status?"

"I'm landing on top of a building nearby. I got permission to land and we'll be there soon, dude."

"Roger, over and out."

Meanwhile, Talmar and a few medical personnel are racing Alan to the emergency room – Sandra and Brooke followed.

"Status on his heart rate?" asked Talmar.

"A bit slow but still holding on," replied one nurse.

"His breathing?"

"Slow," replied another nurse.

"Give him some extra oxygen stat. Prepare a syringe of norepinephrine – I need two CC's," ordered Talmar.

They brought Alan into the emergency room and started hooking him up to equipment.

"Get the I.V. hooked up," ordered Talmar.

"I'm on it."

"Someone get some of the universal Najanian anti-toxin."

"On my way."

Talmar continued to give out orders to medical personnel to try and keep Alan alive. A doctor came and asked Sandra and Brooke to wait outside the emergency room. Sandra started to cry while Brooke tried to comfort her – Lucky caught up.

"Finally, I found you guys. Man, that was a lot of stairs to go down."

Lucky walked over to Sandra and Brooke.

"What I miss?"

"Talmar is working hard in there. We're hoping Al will be alright," said Brooke.

"I know he'll pull through – He's got to – He's the main protagonist."

"Guys, I can't tell you how worried I am – I'm so nervous," cried Sandra.

"Don't worry, Talmar will not stop until the situation is under control," said Brooke.

Suddenly, the rest of the team showed up. Marc, Charles, and Evan guided everyone else down to the emergency area.

"What's the status?" asked Marc.

"Will Alan be okay?" asked Charles.

"Guys, Talmar is still working hard in there with many doctors and nurses. It may take a while," said Brooke.

After fifteen minutes, Talmar came out and faced everyone.

"Alright everyone, may I have your attention please?"

"Will he be okay, Talmar?" asked Sandra.

"Let's talk in the conference room – I have much to explain."

A few nurses roll Alan down the hall to the elevator heading up to the ICU. Talmar asked everyone to follow him to the conference room further down the hall.

Everyone gathered in the room and took a seat. Talmar stood up front and prepared to speak.

"Alright everyone, settle down for a moment. I want to discuss with you what is going on."

The room went silent. Everyone focused on Talmar.

"At the moment, Alan is alright, however, he needs to remain in ICU for maybe a few days. The venom has done a lot of damage to his bodily tissues and it will take a while for him to get back up to par. He's not in critical condition but more in the area of moderate. This doesn't mean he's home free yet nor does this mean he has limited time to live. It just means that we have to hope everything turns out okay."

Talmar paused for a moment.

"We also patched up serious wounds and administered antibiotics. He did have a bit of blood loss – Fortunately, that's the smallest of the problems. Alan is currently semi-conscious and we don't know if he'll fully recover."

The room went silent for a brief moment. Many pondered about what could be done.

"Is there anything that can be done?" asked Brooke.

"I'm not sure," replied Talmar.

Suddenly, Luna, the female gargoyle, which Alan met with a couple of days ago, came in.

"May I suggest a solution?" she asked.

"Luna?" said Brooke.

"It's been a while, Brooke – Good to see you."

Luna moved further into the room.

"Let me introduce myself. My name is Luna. I met your friend and talked to him about what was going on with the invasion. After hearing your friend had been poisoned by Mantor, I brought with me this potion."

Luna took out a small bag with a flask containing a glowing blue liquid in it.

"In this Quartz flask, it is a potion created by a shaman I know. This potion would be able to rejuvenate your friend's health. However, there is a catch. The only way for this potion to work is for it to be distributed by someone who loves him. Do any one of you girls in this room love him?"

"You mean like as a friend?" asked Rebekah.

"I think she means like-like him," said Laura.

Brooke, Talmar, and Lucky turned to Sandra. She timidly raised her hand and then everyone else started to look at her.

"Don't be shy, dear. Do you really have feelings for him?" asked Luna.

Sandra nodded yes and grinned a bit.

"Come with me."

Luna and Sandra exited the room. Talmar informed everyone he'd be right back. They proceeded to the elevator and went to level two.

"This way ladies…" said Talmar.

Talmar brought them to the ICU and showed them to Alan.

"Sandra, I know if there is anything more powerful than medicine, it's love," said Talmar.

Talmar stepped back and moved over to the main desk.

"Sandra, I sense your heart yearns for him – I can see it within you," said Luna

"Alan's a really nice guy. I really care about him."

"Now I want you to listen to what I'm about to tell you. In order for this potion to work, you must do this correctly."

"Okay."

"First, you must give him this entire potion – Every last drop. Lastly, show how much you love him – Your souls must touch."

"Okay."

Sandra walked over to the left side of Alan and sat down in a chair. She opened the flask and prepared to give it to him.

"Alan…"

He was very weak and could barely open his eyes.

"I have something for you to drink. This will help you – I'm going to lift your head up so you can drink it."

Sandra helped Alan lift his head and placed the bottle to his lips. He slowly sipped away at the potion. After finishing, he fell into a deep sleep.

"Is that normal for him to fall asleep like that?" asked Sandra.

"Yes – The shaman said that the one who drinks it may fall into a deep sleep but not to worry," replied Luna.

Sandra held Alan's hand and started petting his head. She moved closer and spoke,

"Alan, if you can hear me, I want you to know how awesome of a guy you are. Once I laid eyes on you, I saw deep within how much a good-hearted person you are. You and I connected so well – It was amazing. I really enjoy your company and I want to continue to get to know you. You've shown me there are miracles, and you have given me hope. You helped defeat Mantor and you have also saved us. You're a hero, Alan. Most of all, you're my hero. You have given me a reason to live – You are my guardian angel. I'm thankful for what you've done for us and we're all proud of you. If there is anything in this world you deserve, you deserve to live and be happy with friends who care about you and who are there for you."

Sandra shed a few tears. Luna, Talmar, and the medical staff were touched by Sandra's words.

"There is no one else in this world I'd rather be with than you, Alan. Even your friends want you to be alright. I know there's nothing more they would want than to see their best friend alive and well."

Sandra embraced him. She held his head close to hers and whispered in his ear,

"I love you, Alan, I really do."

Sandra gave Alan a kiss on his cheek and then kissed his hand.

"Please be okay."

Monitors began showing signs of improvement. Talmar came over to analyze the situation.

"My God, it actually is working. His heart rate is normal, blood pressure is stabilizing, breathing is normal. Brilliant," said Talmar.

Luna patted Sandra on the back – Talmar came over.

"Sandra, stay right here. I'm going to inform everyone of the good news."

Talmar left and proceeded to the elevator in excitement. While he went down to the conference room, Sandra sat next to Alan, gazed at him, and gently caressed his face while she waited – the potion had worked.

"Luna, thank you for your help. I'm so happy he's okay."

"With the many elements and forces surrounding us, love is the most powerful force in this world – So powerful, evil could never out match it."

"Totally."

"It is time for me to go. I bid you well, dear, for happiness can only grow if you give it love and time. By the way, I believe your friend had dropped this."

Luna gave Sandra the Guardian Emblem.

"Farewell, Sandra."

Luna left the ICU and after a few minutes Alan woke up. Queue first-person mode! Whoosh!

* * * * * * *

I awoke and found myself in the hospital. My eyes were a bit blurred but then cleared up. I looked to my left and saw Sandra, petting my head, and smiling her sweet smile.

"Sandra? What happened? How did I get to the hospital?" I asked.

"Lucky and Roller were able to pilot a couple of helicopters and fly you here. Some of us were on the one piloted by Lucky and the rest were on the other with Roller."

"Wow, they could pilot an aircraft?"

"Yep, and they did it quite well. Most of all, Alan, I'm so glad you are okay."

Sandra and I hugged each other tightly. Feeling her arms around me made me feel happy. I really could feel how much she cared about me. Both of us cried during our embrace.

"Oh, Alan, I thought I'd lost you. Thank God you're alright."

Sandra and I held each other a little longer, comforting one another, letting ourselves know everything will be okay. A few minutes later, Marc came in with Lucky, Evan, Charles, and Chris. Only a few visitors at a time could come in.

"Hey guys," I greeted.

"So, how are you feeling?" asked Marc.

"Yeah – We almost lost you, man," Charles added.

"I'm feeling okay."

"Man, you kicked a lot of ass today," said Evan.

"Yeah – You put up a good fight," said Chris

"Hey, where did Luna go?" asked Lucky.

"She left a few minutes ago," Sandra replied.

"Dammit, I wanted to ask her for her number."

"Luna? Was she here? That lizard woman wasn't with her was she?" I asked.

"Lizard woman?" asked Sandra.

"During the evening when Luna spoke with Alan, a lizard woman, who was part of her group, was trying to hit on him. Don't worry, nothing else happened," said Chris.

"Man, I should have asked Luna for *her* number," said Lucky.

"Oh, Alan, Luna found this and wanted me to give it to you," said Sandra.

"The Guardian Emblem..."

    Sandra gave me the necklace and I thanked her – I put it in my pocket for safe keeping. After the little talk with my friends, they left and went back to Brooke's apartment to stay for the night. Talmar stood by in the hospital to monitor my condition. He told me I would be released tomorrow. Later that evening, Sandra came to visit one last time.

"Hey Alan, just wanted to visit you one more time."

    Sandra came over to the bedside.

"I wanted to wish you good night. We'll be back tomorrow morning."

"Everyone is staying at the apartment, right?"

"Yeah – Brooke made enough room for everyone so we could all be comfortable."

"Good – It's going to be nice to have everything go back to normal... or close to normal."

Sandra giggled a bit. She caressed my face and then kissed me on my forehead. I grinned and looked into her eyes. We wished each other a good night. She waved goodbye and blew a kiss. I waved back and smiled. Resting my head on the pillow, I went to sleep. I surely did face the ultimate challenge but I couldn't have survived without the help from my friends.

JOURNEY BACK HOME
19

Morning came and I awoke feeling better than yesterday. A few nurses were talking at the main ICU desk. After about a minute, one came over to me.

"Good morning, Alan. How are you feeling today?"

"I'm feeling fine, thank you."

"Dr. Monitor will be here shortly to do some final examinations on you. In the meantime, would you like something to eat?"

"Sure."

"We have a breakfast tray with eggs and toast – On the side, we have juice and a hot beverage. Would you like tea or coffee?"

"I'll have tea, please."

"Okay, we'll have it sent to you shortly."

"Thank you."

After five minutes, Talmar came through the door and proceeded over to me.

"Good morning Alan, how are you feeling today?"

"I'm doing alright, Talmar. I heard you are going to do some final tests?"

"Correct – I'm just going to make sure every bodily activity is functioning properly so you will be able to leave the hospital today."

"Cool."

"By the way, did you want breakfast?"

"They'll be sending up a breakfast tray shortly."

"Excellent – By the way, Sandra told me how happy she was that you were doing well," started Talmar, "I haven't seen Sandra this happy since she was six years old. Brooke and I are proud of you. You have made Sandra feel happy again. For twelve years Sandra has been in a rut – It was hard for her to feel good about anything – You've set her heart free and given her joy."

"I'm glad – Sandra is such a sweet girl and she deserves to feel happy. She has good karma and bad things should never happen to someone like her. Really, she deserves good things."

"Well, she already has received one good thing, one she is very proud to have met."

"Me?"

Talmar nodded yes.

"The most rewarding thing to anyone is to have great friends by their side. Sandra, most of all, is glad to have you by her side."

I was quite happy to hear this news. As soon as Talmar and I finished our conversation, the breakfast tray had arrived. He let me eat before proceeding to do the tests. In the meantime, he went over to the nurse's station and talked with personnel.

After I finished eating, Talmar came over and proceeded to do the tests. Everything turned out all right and he began preparing a release form.

"Alright Alan, about nine o'clock you should be clear to go. The nurses will disconnect you from the machines and help you get dressed," said Talmar.

"Sounds good."

Shortly after, a couple of nurses came over and started to disconnect the equipment from me. The most uncomfortable part was the removal of the I.V. Having a little annoying needle being removed felt like a never-ending blood test. After everything had been removed, one of the nurses helped me up.

"Alright, Alan, I'll take you to a room where you can get dressed – Follow me."

The nurse escorted me to this small room about the size of a fitting room in a clothing store. I went in and closed the door. It only took me a moment to get dressed. They gave me a white T-shirt since mine had been ripped off me. I exited the cubicle and the nurse brought me to a conference room. When she opened the door, my friends were waiting inside.

"There's big Al," said Charles.

My friends cheered as I entered the room. Sandra came over and gave me a big hug. We all sat down and talked a little. Brooke mentioned Sandra, Talmar, and himself packed up some clothes and possessions. He figured it would be best to get rid of his apartment and start a new life in the human world. While my friends told me what happened after I lost consciousness, there was a knock on the conference room door. The door opened and there stood a tan lizard man dressed in a suit.

"Greetings, ladies, and gentlemen. For those who are humans, I am the Anthronian President."

Fascinated to see the leader of the island pop in, my friends and I were curious about what he had to say.

"Who is the leader of this fine team?" he asked.

I got up from my chair and stood attentively.

"I am, sir."

"I do say I'm quite honored to be in your presence, young man. I thank you for stopping Mantor and bringing his corrupt plot to a halt. Anthronian police have arrested him and he is now in custody."

"Don't thank me, sir, thank my friends. Without them, I would have failed to stop him. Most of all, I thank my team for their efforts and quick thinking for getting me to this hospital. If they weren't here, I'd be dead right now."

"Seeing how you all worked together so well, both human and non-human individuals alike, it shows we *can* get along peacefully. I'm quite convinced this is a start of a new era – An era where humans and our kind can finally live in peace and put our differences aside."

The Anthronian President shook my hand.

"Son, I'm very impressed how you lead your team this far to bring justice to a madman. I feel like a fool for trusting Mantor. Anyway, I will let the guards at the other facilities in your territory release your kind."

"Thank you, sir."

"I will take Mantor's former minions and force them to assist cleaning up the mess made in your territory. It will be something like community service for them."

"Sounds good."

"Thank you again. I'll have a few of my men get a transport vehicle ready and fly all of you back to where you live."

"Thank you, sir," I said, shaking his hand again.

Afterwards, Talmar came back and informed us everything is okay and we are clear to go. A few of the president's guards came in and escorted us out to a few large van-like vehicles. We were on our way to the landing field on the west side of the island. When we arrived, a few of the cages we saw on the east portion of the island were being dropped off. The soldiers opened each and every cage letting all the people out. Then they boarded the huge cruisers.

The vans came to a stop near this fairly sized flying craft. It looked like a Chinook helicopter but instead of it having propellers, it had two sets of jet motors. One set in the front and one set in the back. I turned to Sandra, Brooke, and Talmar.

"Are you sure you guys want to come with us?" I asked.

"We're quite sure, Alan. We are a team, after all, right?" Sandra answered.

"Where ever you go, we go, too," Brooke added.

"Plus, I do want to teach human doctors our medical knowledge and techniques we practice here on Anthronia," added Talmar.

We went aboard the aircraft and took off. I was anxious to get home, find my mother, and live a normal life – or as close to normal as it can get.

After an hour flight, we landed at AOK airport. The landing field still seemed to be quiet but I knew around the world, people were being released and the nightmare had come to an end.

"Home sweet home," said Rebekah.

"Thank God," said Jason.

"Can't wait to go home and relax," said Marc.

"Wasn't our home trashed from the invasion?" asked Laura.

"Ah Shh… Sugar Honey Iced Tea."

We all headed back into the facility and made our way to the main entrance. Thankfully, Marc's van was still there, however, there was one major issue – we could not fit everyone.

"Alan, we may have a capacity issue," said Marc.

"I see."

"Hey, what about that vehicle?" asked Evan.

He pointed to a flipped over shuttle bus on the sidewalk. If we could get it standing upright, we should be able to get it rolling.

"Okay, we need to get this bus standing up. Brooke, would you be able to assist us in lifting it?" I asked.

"Sure thing."

"Evan and Charles, help Brooke."

The three went over to the bus and prepared to lift from the roof. On the count of three, they lifted it with ease. Most of the lifting power, as everyone probably guessed, came from Brooke. With the bus now standing upright, Marc went inside to see if he would be able to start it.

"Hey guys, the keys are still in the ignition," said Marc.

"Alright," said Charles.

"Let's get this baby rolling," said Evan.

Marc got it started and we went aboard the bus.

"Alright everyone, we're going home," said Marc.

Finally, we were on our way back to Levittown to hopefully go back to normal lives. I sat down a few rows back from the front of the bus and I made myself comfortable – Sandra came over and joined me.

"So, how does it feel to be in New York?" I asked.

"A little different but I think I can get used to it," she replied.

We smiled at each other for the moment and then Lucky came over.

"Yo Al, I'm curious, if we are going to be staying with you guys, who are we going to stay with?" asked Lucky.

"Dude, do you have a basement?" asked Roller.

"No, I don't, sadly. My house doesn't have a basement," I replied.

"Damn," said Lucky.

"If you guys want to stay at my house, I could make arrangements. I can only take two or three of you," I said.

"Can my brother and I stay with you? We'll clean up after ourselves," asked Lucky.

"Can I stay with you, too?" asked Sandra.

"I need to ask my mother to make sure it's okay. For the time being, yes, you may."

"Please convince her – We have no other place to stay," said Lucky.

"Don't worry, I'll negotiate something with her."

"Alan, I don't mean to cut in on your conversation but I am curious where the rest of us will be staying," said Talmar.

"Hey, I can take one more in," started Charles, "Brooke, if you want, I have an extra bedroom in my house."

"Do you have a crazy family?"

"Not anymore. My annoying and crazy brother got kicked out of the house and his room will be vacant."

"Yeah, I guess I'll go for it. What do I have to lose?"

"Is there anyone who would like to take me in?" asked Talmar.

"Talmar, I could take you in," started Marc, "I have some space available in my basement. Hopefully, my mom and dad won't have any issues."

"Thank you, Marc. I promise I won't get in the way."

After we discussed where everyone will be placed, we arrived back at Marc's house.

"Whose house is this?" asked Lucky.

"This is my house. It is also where our adventure started."

"Man, there's tons of destruction around here," said Brooke.

"My goodness..." said Talmar.

"This is horrible. I could imagine how horrifying it was for all of you," said Sandra.

"Dude," Roller added.

Before we entered Marc's house, we hung outside for a moment.

"Alan, should we have everyone wait here or bring everyone home?" asked Marc.

"I think it would be best if we stay here. It has been a long adventure and we're all exhausted," I replied.

"Yeah, saving the world can really tire you out," Chris added.

We went inside and made ourselves comfortable. Marc and Laura prepared some snacks and grabbed some sodas from the fridge to bring down into the basement.

"Hey, guys – Got some chips, pretzels, and popcorn. A feast fit for heroes," said Marc.

"Got some soda, too, guys," Laura added.

"Yo Laura, can you toss me a seltzer?" asked Charles.

"Here you go, Chuck."

Marc pulled out some folding chairs since we couldn't all fit on the couch. I cleared off the coffee table to make room for the bowls of snacks we had. We sat down and made a toast with our soda cans.

"Guys, I'd like to make a toast. I want to thank all of you for the incredible teamwork and for being awesome friends – To friendship."

"Cheers."

I pulled out the Guardian Emblem from my pocket and looked at it for a moment.

"Guys, as some of you know, Luna gave this necklace to me. Even though it was bestowed upon me, I believe you all deserve this."

"What is that for, anyway?" asked Chris.

"It is a symbol of truth, justice, and hope. These were worn by a group of heroes known as The Guardians. They came together to fight evil and create peace."

"Kinda sounds like us, right?" said Lucky.

"Maybe we're The Guardians two-point 'O', dude," said Roller.

"Whatever we are, we all are heroes – Your everyday average person," I said.

"Cheers."

Later in the afternoon, Jason, Rebekah, Laura, Evan, Charles, Brooke, and Talmar dozed off. Marc went to go get a couple of inflatable beds and some blankets so there would be enough room for everyone to sleep. As night fell, Chris, Bill, and I placed some lanterns and candles around the house to light the area a bit.

"Marc, would it be alright if I can use your shower?" I asked.

"Sure – That's actually a good idea – After what we've been through – Wouldn't mind taking a shower myself."

"Yeah, after you're done, I'll probably take a shower, too," said Bill.

"If he takes more than fifteen minutes, he's doing more than taking a shower, man…" said Lucky.

"I'll only be ten minutes tops."

"We'll be timing you…" said Mike, teasing me.

I went upstairs and grabbed a towel from the linen closet. Entering the bathroom, I made sure the faucet still worked. Fortunately, the water system was fine. I took my shower and washed off all the dirt I had on me. After I finished, I dried off, got dressed, and went back downstairs.

"If anyone else wants to take a shower, the bathroom is free."

"I'll go," said Bill.

"After Bill, I'll go. I feel so disgusting not bathing after three days," said Chris.

"I'm going to have a little tea. Do any of you want?"

"I'll have," Marc replied.

"Me, too," Sandra added.

"What tea would you like?"

"I'll have whatever you're having," Sandra replied.

"I'll have Earl Grey," Marc replied.

I went up to Marc's kitchen and took out three cups. Fortunately, the water cooler had a battery back-up. He installed it just in case there's a power outage lasting for a week. This made it a lot easier to prepare the tea. I pulled out the box of tea bags Marc had in the pantry and took out one Earl Grey and two green tea bags. I prepared the tea and I brought down Marc's and Sandra's. As I went back up to get mine, Sandra followed me.

"Hey Sandra, did you want some sugar or honey for your tea?"

"No, thank you."

Sandra sat down at the kitchen table sipping her tea. I sat down across from her. Candles illuminated the kitchen. The flames danced and gave a romantic aura.

"This kinda feels romantic with all these candles lying about," said Sandra.

"Yeah, you're right."

Sandra and I gazed at each other. She put her hand out and touched my face. She gently caressed me while staring deep into my eyes. I placed my hand over hers, acknowledging her feelings for me.

"You are one of the most wonderful guys I've ever met – I don't know what I would've done if I lost you, Alan."

We stared at each other a moment longer. I thought we would eventually kiss – the moment was perfect for it. Over by the kitchen entrance, we heard something. Apparently Lucky and Roller were having a sibling rivalry moment.

"Dude, you messed up the moment," said Roller.

"Maybe if you weren't pushing me, I would've been quieter." said Lucky.

"What are you guys doing?" I asked.

"Well, since the two of you were sitting there looking like you were about to kiss, I didn't want to miss that, man."

"Sandra and I were just enjoying tea together."

"Yeah, tell me those long stares are nothing. I know you two are smitten."

I looked at Sandra and she looked at me.

"Hey Luck, tell you what, after everything is settled, maybe Alan and I will go out on a date."

"You hear that, Alando? You better ask her out – Don't worry, Sandra, I'll turn your boy into a man."

Sandra and I finished our tea. We went back down to the basement and got ready for bed. Before I went to sleep, I wanted to check my laptop to see how much power remained in the battery.

"Is that your laptop?" asked Sandra.

"Yes – I was working on a story before the invasion hit."

"You write?"

"Yeah – Take a look..."

"Let's see... Hey, maybe you can take our adventure and write a story about it."

"Not a bad idea..."

After ten minutes, I turned off my laptop and hopped onto one of the inflatable beds – Sandra slept next to me. We wished each other a good night, pulled the blanket over us, and closed my eyes. After a couple of minutes, I felt her putting her arm across my chest and getting close to me. She began petting my right arm. I started to feel like a teddy bear since I seemed to be like a security blanket to her – more like a security human. I opened my eyes and saw her, sound asleep and cuddling with me. She rested near my neck and I could feel her breathing. Despite it may seem a little weird for the first thirty seconds, I thought this wasn't so bad after all. It was pleasant to see her calm and enjoying a relaxing slumber. I took my right hand and started to pet her left arm. My eyes grew heavy and I slowly dozed off.

FINALE
20

As morning came, I awoke and saw Sandra still sleeping next to me. Lucky and Roller were up and stared at me with big smiles.

"So Al, get any last night?"

"Anything interesting happen, dude?"

"Guys, we didn't *do* anything," I said.

"Just look at her, she's all over you, man," chuckled Lucky.

"Dude, are you hungry?"

"Yeah, let's go raid Marc's fridge."

"Don't make a mess guys."

Lucky and Roller went upstairs to get something to eat. I turned to check on Sandra. She was moving a bit and then slowly opened her eyes.

"Good morning," I said.

"Good morning," she replied.

Sandra smiled at me.

"That was one of the best night sleeps I had in a long time," said Sandra.

Sandra and I stared at each other. After a moment, there was a knock at the door – Lucky called down.

"Hey Alando, there's a couple of dudes in black suits and sunglasses outside," called Lucky.

"Hang on a second," I replied.

Sandra and I got out of bed. I went to wake up Marc and asked him to come with me upstairs to check out our visitors. He followed and answered the door.

"May I help you, gentlemen?"

"Hi, I'm special agent Jackson from the FBI. Can all of you come with us, please?"

"May I ask why?"

"The President of the United States would like to see you."

"Seriously?"

"Yes."

"Alright, can you give us twenty minutes? We just got up."

The service agent said okay to our request – wouldn't want to meet the President in our pajamas. We woke everyone up and told them who had requested us. After we got ready, we left the house and went aboard a limo the FBI had provided.

They brought us to AOK airport where they had a large private jet waiting. We went aboard it and flew down to Washington D.C. From there, we were escorted to the White House via limo and then brought inside. We would never have imagined stepping foot in the White House. Secret Service agents escorted us to the President's office. Behind the desk sat the President of the United States. He turned around in his chair and greeted us.

"Welcome," started the President, "I have to say I'm honored to meet a group of young people who sacrificed their lives to save millions. Who is the leader of this group?"

"I am, sir," I said.

"What's your name, young man?"

"My name is Alan, sir."

"Alan, I have to say you did a fine job leading your team to save humanity. Also, your efforts have brought peace between our world and that island in the Atlantic, Antonio."

"It's Anthronia, sir," I corrected.

"Right – Anyway, your efforts have brought peace. You did a fine job."

"I appreciate the thanks, sir, but it wasn't just me, you also have to thank my friends. I would not be here without them. These guys deserve every ounce of credit."

"I say you are very lucky you have friends who care about you."

"Believe me, the one thing I'm most proud of having *are* my friends. They are my dream team."

"And you've turned them into heroes."

"I guess I have, sir."

"Son, as a reward for the efforts that you and your team have shown, I gift you all…"

The President began pulling something out of his suit pocket. What could it be? Money? Medals of Honor? We were very anxious to find out.

"… these gift cards to an ice cream shop so you all can celebrate with refreshing ice cream."

We were silent and looked down at the gift cards. We did not save the world to deserve this. I knew my friends were just as disappointed as I was.

"I hope you can use these, I got these as gifts and I never got a chance to use them."

"Mister President, we appreciate your offer but…" I started to say.

"Are you kidding? This is what we get for risking our asses?" exclaimed Charles.

"Are you trying to rip us off?" Jason added.

"Come on, old gift cards? What the hell?" exclaimed Evan.

"Mister President, this is outrageous – Surely we deserve better – For what we went through..." said Marc.

"This is bull crap," exclaimed Charles.

"Guys," I shouted, "Calm down, please."

Everyone quieted down.

"Alan, we deserve something better than this. You're not thinking of accepting these, are you?" asked Chris.

"No, I'm not, Chris. I'm going to discuss the issue peacefully with the President."

I prepared to speak to the President. I know for sure my friends deserve something a whole lot better than gift cards. They deserved something signifying their efforts in sacrificing their lives and saving lives of others.

"Mister President, I'm sorry to say, but we will not accept your gift cards. I appreciate the thought but quite frankly, these gift cards do not signify the heroics my friends and I performed for the past few days."

"Well, what would you want?"

"Sir, what I want for my team to have is recognition. My friends deserve Medals of Honor for their heroics and their bravery."

"Medals of Honor? I give those to the military."

"Sir, your infantry failed to keep back the invaders. We were able to break through their defenses and infiltrate the villain's lair. We did a lot more than what your guys did," said Evan.

"Yeah," Charles added.

"Mister President, I suggest you give these guys medals. Without them, you and the rest of humankind would not be here alive," said Brooke.

"Wow, I didn't know you guys talked."

"Mister President, even though we may not be human, we still are able to speak fluent English," said Talmar.

"Okay, tell ya what, I'll get you guys those pedals but for now, how about a vacation spot in the Bananas where you can all relax for a couple of days. Does that sound good?"

Despite the President lacked the ability to speak correctly, I huddled with my buddies and briefly discussed the offer. We all agreed to it and I prepared to tell the President.

"Mister President, we will accept your offer for the vacation spot."

"Excellent – After we get all the people back to their homes and after we clean up the mess that was made, I'll invite you all back here to give you your medals. Sound good?"

"Thank you, sir," I said, thinking to myself this guy is an idiot.

"I'll get a couple of my guys to prepare a plane to fly you all down to the vacation spot. Take care and we'll keep you posted... stay the course..."

We left his office and went back down to the limo. A lot of us were quite bummed out the President had the audacity to pull that crap.

"I tell you he is a dumb ass, man," said Lucky.

"More like a candy ass bitch," Evan added.

"I'm starting to feel respect for the Anthronian President," said Brooke.

"How does a politician like himself get that job? It looks like he has no idea what he is doing," said Talmar.

"Dumb luck," I answered.

"Most people voted for the other guy during the elections but somehow this moron won," said Marc.

"Sounds like someone tampered with your votes," said Brooke.

"Dude," Roller added.

"Hey guys, since we're like a super team, we need to call ourselves something. Maybe League of Heroes," said Lucky.

"How about The Guardians just like in the legend..." said Marc.

"Dude, how about the Super Dudes..." said Roller.

"How about Fighting Fortress..." said Jason.

"Nah, how about Super Squad..." said Rebekah.

"Man, I was thinking of Gangsta Force," said Evan.

"How about Justice Squad..." said Charles.

"How about The Fantastic Fifteen..." said Laura.

"All sound cool but, what about Paranormal Investigation Agency?" I suggested.

"What's so paranormal about the adventure?" asked Brooke.

"We've faced Hell spawns," I replied.

"Maybe something that deals with the public," said Chris.

"Protecting the public..." Bill added.

"Maybe Public Protection Squad..." said Mike.

"Public Protection Team..." said Sandra.

"Wait, I've got it – The Public Protection Agency," I said.

"Brilliant," said Talmar.

"We shall be known as the Public Protection Agency," said Marc.

"For short, the PPA," said Charles.

    The FBI agents brought us to the airport and we went aboard the jet. They said they will inform our loved ones we were okay. We flew off to the Bahamas and started our vacation at this beach house. Once settled, my friends started to enjoy themselves. I sat outside and watched the sunset. The cool breeze helped me relax. I got up and went over to the end of the deck. My arms rested on the railing, looking out over the ocean. Sandra came out and walked over to me.

"Hey, Alan," said Sandra, "Don't you want to come in and celebrate?"

"I'll do that shortly. I just needed some fresh air."

"Such a beautiful sunset."

"Indeed, it is."

"Back on Anthronia, I used to head down to the beach and look at the sun setting. I went to the beach to escape the stress of everyday living."

There was a brief pause. The sound of the waves crashing on the shore echoed. Sandra turned to me and smiled – she moved closer to me. We looked out over the ocean for a moment. Sandra put her arm around my shoulder and pulled me closer to her. Then we heard the click sound of a camera. Looking back, we saw Lucky taking a picture of us.

"Gotcha," said Lucky.

"Lucky…" I started to say.

"Come on, get close now… yeah, now smile."

Sandra and I got close together. She put her left arm around my shoulder and held me with her right arm. Lucky snapped the picture.

"You two look good together, you know that?"

I started to blush.

"I'm serious man – She's all over you."

We all had a little laugh. Sandra gazed at me and we both smiled at each other.

"Now let's head inside and party," said Sandra.

"Yeah, baby – Wooo," shouted Lucky.

Sandra held my hand as we were going inside. A nice slow-paced song played in the background.

"Would you like to dance?" she asked.

"I'd be delighted, Sandra," I said, confidently.

We started to dance slowly and, as the night went on, we all had a good time. This vacation was well deserved.

By the time our vacation ended, we went home and those, including myself, who had special guests, needed to persuade our parents into letting them stay. When I saw my mother, she was so happy to see me. I told her about my new friends and how they helped me out. My mother seemed a bit reluctant at first. Once I told her what Sandra did for me, she then said okay. Lucky, Roller, and Sandra were allowed to stay. My mom set some ground rules and what is to be expected.

The rules are as follows:

1. When it is time for bed, they must be quiet and go to sleep.
2. If they make a mess, they must clean it up.
3. Sandra is not allowed to sleep in the same bed as Alan.
4. All three must bathe often.
5. They must respect any guests that come over and not to freak them out.
6. They must also help clean around the house.

Those are pretty much the rules my mom gave them. I know Sandra is going to miss sleeping next to me but at least she can stay in the same room.

At Marc's house, he told me he had minimal issues persuading his parents. Since Talmar is well-mannered and very civilized, Marc's folks were quite pleased. Laura, too, does not mind Talmar staying with them.

At Charles' house, he told me it wasn't too bad. He had to do a lot of persuading but at least his parents came through, especially after they saw Brooke's impressive strength – in other words, his parents found a use for him around the house.

Within a week, Brooke went back to Anthronia to get any remaining belongings he had in his apartment. He brought some of Sandra's items to my house and some of Talmar's to Marc's. When Brooke dropped by, he was glad to see Sandra happy. I could see it in his glowing, head-light eyes – a guy who has seen his friend suffer for so long now feeling happier than ever.

We all went back to our normal routines and helped one another fix up each other's house. Since the natives of Anthronia came to our area, they started helping everyone. Everything got repaired faster and more efficiently. Since a friendly bond existed between humans and the Anthronia natives, the likelihood of another war was slim.

My friends and I enjoyed every bit of the positives after the invasion. After three months, the President invited us back to Washington D.C. to receive our Medals of Honor. The ceremony took place in front of the White House. Our friends and family attended the affair. Other spectators were present and it too, was being televised. One by one, the President called us up to get our medals. Afterwards, he gave a small speech:

"My fellow Americans and those who may be watching around the world, we have been through rough times and this most recent catastrophic event being the most terrifying. In the many years of seeing what our troops have been through in Iraq and Afghanistan and seeing all sorts of other chaos, never in my lifetime have I seen such courage and valor from these fine young people next to me. Because of their heroic acts, this invasion has ceased and the war has ended. Not to mention millions of innocent lives were saved because of our heroes here. Ladies and gentlemen, I present to you our guardian angles, the Public Protection Agency."

I could see in the distance my mother shedding tears of joy. I looked to my left and saw Sandra looking back at me smiling. As the ceremony ended, Marc put his arm around me from the right and Charles put his arm around me from the left. I put my arms around both of them. As we were walking over to our friends and family, Charles began to sing the tune from Queen's "We are the Champions." Then Marc, myself, Evan, Mike, Lucky, Roller, Laura, and Jason joined in. It was an epic ending to the day.

Back at my house, I hung out with Sandra, Lucky, and Roller. Before going to bed, we talked a bit.

"I can't believe we got medals, man," said Lucky.

"Dude, this is awesome."

"This was some adventure, right guys?" said Sandra

"Yeah..." I said, with hesitation.

"You okay, Alan?" Sandra asked.

"I'm just a little concerned about something that's been bothering me. Even though we beat Mantor, Sphinx is still on the loose. Does anyone even know what happened to her?"

"All we know is that she had vanished into the vegetation," said Lucky.

"Looks like we'll have to be on high alert. Knowing her, she may seek revenge."

"Don't worry, dude. There's fifteen of us and one of her."

"We'll be ready for her..." said Sandra.

"We will win..." said Lucky.

    I looked at my friends and smiled. I knew I could always count on them to help me get through any situation. When fighting alongside them, I know we're not only just friends – we are a team of heroes.

We are the Public Protection Agency!

THE END

A STORY TWELVE YEARS IN THE MAKING...

<u>Adventures of the PPA: Invasion</u> started out as an idea back in 2005. One day at school, I was talking to my friend Chris. We were in the weight room during gym class and the idea just hit me. I told him I wanted to write a novel. At the time, I was into writing short stories. My friends knew I had a wild imagination and all the things I came up with were out of this world. When I first wrote the story back in 2005, it was a lot different than the final version you see before you. This story has gone through many changes over the years and now it has been polished up and ready to be seen by the world.